BORN TO BE LOVED

I0674452

by

CHARLES NUETZEL

WRITING AS "FRED DAVIS"

The Borgo Press
An Imprint of Wildside Press

MMVII

Dedicated to
A Damsel (who was) in distress—
But is now doing just fine!

SECOND EDITION

CONTENTS

INTRODUCTION

This is the story of a young man seeking a second chance in life, a new beginning. And when his uncle Ben offers him a job in Hollywood, he leaps at the chance.

That is basically the concept that I started out with in writing this book.

For some reason I especially liked the opening of the book. It is a scene where we meet our hero, and learn something about his background and attitude towards women.

The setting is a small motel at a tiny wayside gas-stop in the middle of the California desert. There's a coffee shop and a lonely young waitress tossed in for good measure.

The young lady is a prime example of the girl trapped in a nowhere place, desperately isolated and hungry just to be held, cared for, loved.

What would happen when the two met?

Like I suggest, this is a scene that sets up the character of Johnny, our hero. Nothing more.

James Dean and the young Paul Newman were big in films around the time of the book's original writing. Not that the Johnny in this book was anything as dynamic as either of these actors in real or imagined life. But I kind of think that Johnny might have thought of himself in that way. Lean, attractive to women, young and old. He is, in reality, somewhat of an "escort" for hire, when the story opens. And he wants out of that gig!

So he comes to Hollywood to get a fresh start, after years of living off lonely widows as their paid lover. This was a new beginning; and he is determined to make the most of this chance for a new life, a new beginning.

But, of course, life isn't all that simple.

And so the complications begin!

Things might have worked out, if his uncle's young wife, Laura, hadn't wanted him as a lover. He instantly realized this was another trap!

Uncle Ben was a dangerous and violent man, with underworld connections.

In desperation to break free of Laura, he becomes involved with one of the strippers working for the club, then more seriously with a struggling young actress who has made the wrong kind of films—for his uncle!

But Laura won't stop making demands on him, and all hell breaks loose when Ben discovers the truth!

A novel which exposes the terrible price that life can inflict on people desperate to have a second chance.

—CHARLES NUETZEL
Thousand Oaks, California
August 2006

CHAPTER ONE

The desert night breeze was hot as it blew through the open window of the small, weathered motel room. The young man slowly slipped under the covers, cursing the necessity of playing out his little game with the young waitress who would soon be arriving with food and probably one hell of a lot more—if he knew women!

Johnny Belmont laughed to himself as the sheets covered his naked flesh. The bedsprings complained as he shifted into a more comfortable sitting position.

"If I know my women, this Mary will be helping me really bang up a racket with this bed!" he chuckled.

A sharp edge of excitement shot through Johnny as he considered the young waitress. She looked like a lonely, sex-starved girl who would serve herself up on a platter for any man willing to share a bed. He had known a lot of girls like her. They lived lonely lives in nowhere places like this road stop, that was nothing more than a gas station, restaurant, and motel dropped between Las Vegas and Los Angeles. He didn't question the fact that when she brought his dinner, it would be with the offer of more than food to devour.

The thought pleased him. She'd probably be the last casual bird to joyride with him. The last of countless women, young and old, rich and poor, who found it difficult to turn down a good-looking stud like Johnny Belmont. He didn't fool himself about the attractiveness of his body or his power over women. That was the only talent he'd ever had; the only complete success he'd managed to rack up on his life chart. It was the one thing he clung to like a desperate, drowning man clutching at a straw in the middle of a pool of quicksand.

There was a timid knock on the motel room door.

Johnny looked at his watch, where it lay on the small stand beside the double bed. It was almost exactly an hour since he had left the restaurant.

A pleased grin spread across his handsome lips.

"Come in," was Johnny's only response.

A brownish-haired woman in her middle twenties stepped in, pushing the door open with her back.

She was still dressed in the slightly wrinkled yellow uniform—but the cap was gone and her hair hung loose in long straight lines about her face and shoulders. Johnny noticed that the top button of the uniform had been opened.

The longing, half-hidden, desperate look in her eyes as they met his revealed naked loneliness, days and weeks without real lovers. Without real human contact. She was one of those typical females lost in nowhere towns, crummy shacks, lousy jobs, and even crammed in the big city crunch of agonized isolation. They were all the same in so many ways. And he'd managed to make the most of their hungers for human connection. They had been easy meat to his seductive powers—and he'd enjoyed all of them.

For a moment a pang of understanding and almost tenderness flashed through Johnny. Sure, he'd known a lot of girls like her, used them for an instant night of pleasure and disappeared. They were born to be used. Just like he had been, as one rich lady claimed, "born to be loved!"

But, Johnny realized, he was just as foolish and lonely and just as much of a failure in life as this woman and many of those before her. To the rich bitches, the high-society tramps, the young girls out for an attractive escort and a big bang-up screwing time in the wee hours of the night, Johnny Belmont had been only a thing to be loved and tossed aside.

Yes, he thought, they were all hungry, lonely and needed love of one kind or another to make it possible to survive another long day.

In a way he had a lot in common with this young waitress. Too much so.

"Hello," she greeted in a slightly timid, shy voice.

There wasn't any real outward embarrassment in her actions as she moved toward the bed with a covered dinner plate, a bottle of whiskey and two glasses. Only those eyes, pleading to give her a moment of escape from this small, closed-in world in which she lived.

"Hi," he grinned as she placed the tray on a narrow desk a few feet from the bed.

She turned, offering: "Drinks, or food first?"

He studied her full body as if he were trying to see through the formless cloth that draped about it.

She had wide hips, a slight belly, and high plump breasts pressing against the half-open top of the uniform. Johnny noticed she'd removed her bra.

This was the last time to enjoy such casual pleasures, he realized, almost sadly. *And against all the beauties I've escorted into bed in the past, this Mary didn't stack up very good.*

"How about drinks?" He hadn't ordered the bottle; she had brought it on her own. "Nice of you to think of it. What will I owe you for it?"

"Oh, forget that!" Mary tossed her head, causing the hair to flow freely about her shoulders.

There was a kind of innocent honesty about this woman that suddenly appealed to Johnny.

It wasn't how beautiful the body might be, he told himself, only how it enjoys mine.

He became aware of the fact that he already was hard against the sheets.

"Where are you heading?" Mary asked, while pouring two strong drinks.

"L.A., have a job offer. Something pretty big," Johnny said absently, watching the suggested form of her fanny as it pushed against the uniform.

Full and plump, Johnny mused. *Something to grip during the hot plunges of passion within that ripe young body.*

Suddenly he realized how hot he was. The drive through the burning desert had created a nagging hunger for a woman.

He had been merely passing through the small wayside three-building settlement. It had seemed to offer nothing but a fast snack meal. The restaurant was in the middle of nowhere, placed down in the desert with a tired gas station and cheaply built motel. Johnny had left his car at the station and gone into the restaurant.

A fast stop before taking the final drive into California.

Once in L.A., things would change for him. His uncle's offer of a job and a new start in life was his only chance of climbing out of the cesspool of being basically a kept stud for rich women. And, he realistically admitted, it wasn't the kind of role a guy could continue enjoying for long; age would, in time, creep up on him. He'd stomped on a lot of gigolos who had outgrown their roles and were merely hanger-ons, desperately attempting to avoid the total defeat their lives had turned into. He didn't want to fall into that trap. Now he had one hope for the future, and he couldn't take a chance on ruining it.

Yet he was in no rush to get caught up in that new life. Who knew when he'd have a chance to hook up with some ripe, hungry broad. The situation was going to be different; and his life-style changed dramatically. So he was open to a little last minute fun.

One look at the young girl standing behind the counter wiping its surface clean and Johnny had felt a prickling sensation knife through him. She wasn't all that beautiful, but still a soft, fleshy woman. She was at least cute enough to make a stopover worthwhile. When she looked up, he knew her whole life story. She was trapped in the middle of nowhere, without enough boyfriends to go around. The way she'd looked over his body and then into his eyes left no doubt that she had to get every kick offered, whenever it came along.

She was lonely, bored, and ready for anything that looked more interesting than the men who lived in this three-building roadside establishment.

"Anything good to eat here, honey?" he inquired, settling in the chair opposite where she was wiping the counter. He let his gaze run invitingly over her figure.

When her eyes met his, he saw the pain again, and the silent cry of desperation that called for help; for escape from a bitter loneliness. She wasn't as attractive up close as she'd been at a distance, but the body was promising.

"Anything you can eat in the breakfast line, mister," she said in a pleasant voice. "Too late for dinner."

His eyes rested on her breasts. "Call me Jack."

"I'm Mary."

"Now we're friends, aren't we?" he gave her that winning grin which had melted many young girls into his arms. The kind of come-on offer that caught even rich bitches into its seductive web. They were all so easy for him.

Turning, he looked at the six-unit motel across the street, next to the gas station.

"You serve meals over there?" His eyes returned to her and lingered on the uniform where it flared out at her hips.

Their gaze met for a brief minute, but it was enough.

"Sure, Jack. Cost a dollar extra, though."

"Could you bring it over? You work here all night?"

"Off in an hour."

"I'm in no hurry. Whenever you get around to it.

Gotta shave, clean up a bit."

He got a room from the gas attendant. After shaving and showering, he'd unlocked the door and then climbed into bed.

Yes, Johnny thought, as Mary moved toward the bed, her hips slightly swaying back and forth with each gliding step, *it just might be real fun spending the night with her.* Girls like Mary were desperate enough to be damned good lays.

"Where are you from?" Mary asked, handing him a whiskey and water.

"Everywhere, mostly."

"What do you do?" she inquired, sitting on the bed next to him, her eyes drifting quickly over the full length of his form under the covers, hesitating at the point where his groin.

"Done a lot of things. And..."

"Bet you've known a lot of women, too" she suggested, raising her own glass to wide, full lips. After sipping the drink, the tip of her tongue licked out slightly, then disappeared. "I needed that."

"I've known a few women in my time."

Her eyes flicked down over his form again as she said:

"I just bet. You're quite a young guy. Aren't you? I mean...bet you're younger than I am!"

"Not that young, I'm afraid," Johnny laughed, amused by her awkward little conversational game. She'd already seen he was hard up for her. And from the lifting and falling of her breasts, it was obvious how hot she was.

"How about you?" he asked, wondering what the answer would be.

"About what?"

"Men."

"Oh, I've known a few in my time," she countered with a quick smile. "A girl gets around. You know how it is."

Her lips were a little too big, but he could easily imagine the sensual delights they could give a man when put in the right places.

"Anything serious?"

"In this place? Are you kidding? Only older guys. You saw the jack at the station. Nothing. And my boss...well, he'd like to have some you know what, but..." She shrugged. Her breast jerked under the uniform. "Most jacks that come around here are just passing through, if you know what I mean."

"Like me? Right?" he offered lightly.

"I suppose so. Maybe not as nice looking."

"Oh?" He was tempted to tease her, to play out a flirtatious game just for the fun of it. But decided against that.

Her eyes were now lowered to where his legs met under the covers. Unconsciously her lips parted and the tip of her tongue quickly moistened their surface.

He could easily guess what was on her mind.

A twitch of automatic excitement snapped him, making the covers jerk slightly.

"How about the food before it gets cold?" she offered.

"Food? Cold? Not important, really. I'm not that hungry for...food. Not that kind, anyway, to be truthful," he quipped.

"You make that sound so...suggestive," Mary observed, eyes probing his.

"Anything wrong with that?" he countered, a

broad grin on his face.

"You're pretty sure of yourself, aren't you?" There wasn't any irritation or anger in her voice.

"Let's consider the facts, honey. You really aren't here only to share a drink with me, are you?"

She ignored his statement, looked down to where his hard erection was so obviously announcing itself.

"You're completely naked, aren't you?"

"What do you think?" He let his hand fall to her thigh. It was soft and full under the skirt of the uniform. Maybe even a little hot. His fingers played upward, teasingly. "You're passionate, really hot!"

"What makes you so sure?" she inquired in a very husky voice.

"Just that I know women." He felt the fullness of the flesh of her upper thigh, squeezing gently. She felt very hot. Even through the clothing.

"Yes, of course, you said there were a lot of women in your life," was her only comment.

They were silent for a long time, drinking, aware of the one physical contact between them. Johnny knew enough to play it at her rate of speed; not that he thought she wouldn't be willing to start immediately. But it would be all the more rewarding at a slow pace. A hot, panting bitch in heat, especially a desperately lonely one, would do anything and everything. And he felt horny as hell and wanted a lot of action out of her ripe young body. Why not; it would feed both of their needs.

When she put her drink—half finished—down on the nightstand, Johnny let his fingers press between her thighs, which quickly parted. The uniform plunged down between her legs, which immediately squeezed together, trapping his fingers.

Then she leaned down, sliding closer. Their lips met, fully open. She thrust a tongue deep within his mouth, swiftly exploring as if tasting a rare wine. His other hand moved up against one of her full breasts, which were now pumping up and down rapidly with her heavy breathing.

As her tongue slowly withdrew, Johnny followed it. She voluptuously sucked on his flesh, pulling his tongue deep into her mouth, as if attempting to swallow its total bulk.

The pressure of a rising nipple revealed that he'd been right about Mary not wearing a bra.

When the kiss broke, both were heavily panting. Mary dropped her hand to his stomach, feeling the firm flat muscles through the covers.

"You're very hard and strong," she stated, gliding her fingers in caressing circles, each one lowering.

"You're big and feel beautiful." Her voice was a low rasp of passionate desire. "It's really large!"

"You look pretty hot and sexy yourself. You've really got some knockers! It felt great, right here in the palm of my hand. Soft and supple. Big, lovely!"

She laughed nervously. "I got boobies, don't I?"

"How about showing them off?"

"All that eager?" she giggled in delight, slowly unbuttoning her uniform. Mary moistened her lips, winked playfully.

As the cloth parted, the crevice between her full, molded breasts appeared like a deep valley surrounded by creamy smooth high hills. When she pulled one arm free of the sleeve, the rosy point of one nipple swelled past the edge of the uniform and

16

was followed by a large, firmly shaped, plump breast. Then she slipped her other arm free, all the time gazing excitedly into his eyes. As the uniform fell about Mary's hips, Johnny gazed hungrily at the two lovely large breasts that supported big, tightly erected pink nipples.

"Man, you sure got 'em!" Johnny exclaimed before taking a quick, hard swallow of his drink. "You got real fancy knockers!"

"You talk funny," she giggled, already obviously high. No doubt she'd had a couple of quick drinks before coming over to the motel room.

"I don't love funny, honey. You can bet your big plump titties on that!"

His hands reached out and folded over each breast, giving them a quick, sensual squeeze. "They're great. Something to really work on!"

"You're crazy!" Mary almost sobbed, her breasts swelling up against the palms of his hands as she sucked in a deep breath. It was almost a gasp of pleasure.

Impulsively, she reached out and pulled the covers away from Johnny's body, down far enough to expose him from the thighs up. Another gasp of delight brought her breasts harder against his hands. He caressed her in circular movements, fondling and squeezing that supple flesh about the hard nipples.

"Boy, you're big!" she half sobbed, hands at him, fingers intertwining so that he was pressed between her soft, delicate, warm palms. She tightened and relaxed her hold on him several times. Then he felt her palms glide up and down, while soft moans of delight uttered from deep within her chest.

"This makes me terribly hot." It was a tortured, throaty comment. He squeezed the rigid points of her nipples with thumb and fingers, lightly pulling on them.

"You got anything under that?" Johnny asked, glancing down at her waist, still covered by the uniform.

"Nothing you don't want, I'm sure!" she almost laughed in happy delight. "Oh, you're fun. Fun. So much fun." At each "fun" her hands had jerked up on him, bringing quick erotic twitches of pleasure. "Bet you really juice a girl up great with this beautiful thing!"

"Keep that up...and you won't get what's coming to you," he pointed out.

"Oh, I bet you would will...again and again. It looks powerful! Like a jack hammer or a wonderful drill...and I've got a well just waiting for it!" She giggled in delight at her verbal statement. "I'm wicked, aren't I?"

They both laughed and released one another.

"You do that pretty good," Johnny pointed out as she started to stand.

"Do what?" her voice asked very innocently, while she worked the uniform down over her hips. "What do I do pretty good?"

"What a sexy body!" Johnny observed. "That's good enough to eat!"

"You want to eat me up? I thought you weren't hungry."

"Well, not for food. Not that kind, anyway!"

"What do you want to...eat?" She giggled in delight, rolling her hips suggestively; "Is that what you want?"

He watched as she slowly lowered her panties down toward full, beefy, cream-colored thighs.

"You work a man over good," he observed as she stepped one leg out of the uniform. "Real good! Soft, hot hands!"

Mary paused long enough to look at him and asked:

"I'm good at playing with it? You sure have a big, fat jack? Is that what you mean?"

"Pretty good, for openers!"

Johnny reached out, letting his hand come between her legs.

"That feels wonderful!" A tremble moved through her body. When he withdrew his hand, she kicked the uniform from her other foot, swiftly slipped onto the bed. She was staring greedily down at him. Her hands gripped the inner curves of his thighs.

"Oh, every muscle is so beautifully hard!" she murmured.

He saw her lips part, open wide, the tip of her tongue reach out, touching their surface. "I like big thick jacks. I just love them up and down, all over the place!"

'What do you like to do with them?" Johnny asked, knowing what was racing through her hot little mind.

His left hand reached under one plump breast, gave it a good, firm squeeze as he slipped the other hand against her fanny, which lifted to make room for him.

"You sure have a great jack," Mary said almost in a whisper, beginning to lean forward, head lowering. "Gee, it's so hot and hard!"

A ripple of excitement jerked through Johnny.

He could already almost feel her hot breath against his groin.

"What's ya gonna do to my jack?" Johnny inquired, teasing her with his fingers, caressing gently against her hot flesh.

In response, Mary lost control and her lips swiftly lowered, greedily enveloping him.

He felt the wiggling movement of her tongue and automatically explored her with quick, gliding caresses.

"You're...really something!" he muttered in tense pleasure as she continued to voluptuously hold him with trembling lips.

Driven to a peak of busting passion, he pulled his hand from under her fanny and then grabbed her soft shoulders.

Mary was yanked away and he dragged that hot naked body across his, thrilling to the body contact.

Her mouth was still open, tongue extended as he covered it with his own. He felt her tense all over as they passionately French-kissed, bodies trembling against one another.

As the kiss broke long enough for breath, Johnny grabbed her hips, pushing them up enough so it was possible to direct himself between her parting thighs.

"Oh," she moaned in immediate pleasure, "do it slow and crazy!"

But there was nothing slow or lingering about their mutual attack.

A mutual gasp of intense pleasure burst from both of them as they experienced first penetration. Her warm, moist flesh had swallowed the full length of him.

Then pure, animal fury drove them wildly at one another, not stopping until they had totally spent one another. .

When climax came, he was overwhelmingly rewarded. He realized this would probably be the last casual sex he would be able to afford. And he planned on enjoying it fully!

She almost screamed in her releasing pleasure and then fell against him, exhausted. They lay there for a long time before moving. Johnny wasn't sure he had fallen asleep or not. Movement brought him to full consciousness. She rolled on her side, facing him. Johnny turned and then smothered himself against her full breasts.

It was late in the morning before they finally tired of each other and Mary fell exhausted on the bed, half drunk and spent by hours of sexual play. She'd really turned herself inside out. It had been a great orgy.

He slipped out of bed, dressed and was about to leave when he glanced at the sleeping form of the young woman.

What the hell, he thought, pulling out the wallet and carefully taking a couple of fives from it to pay for the uneaten food and drinks. He put the money on the tray. Then peeled out another five. Maybe she'd think he considered her a cheap whore, but the money might buy her a new dress or something else. What difference did it make what she thought. The money would be a nice gift to her. After what they'd experienced, she deserved something. And he really didn't need the cash any more. Impulsively he added a couple of twenties.

It was late morning when he entered Beverly Hills. The only regret he had about the future was it wouldn't involve the life-style he'd mastered so well. He was entering the unknown and that was somewhat unnerving.

As he drove down Sunset Boulevard, his mental outlook about the future seemed clouded. There would be his uncle Ben Henderson, and the man's wife. He knew nothing about her other than her name, Laura, and that she was much younger than her husband.

Just for a moment Johnny wondered if he might be making a mistake. He didn't know anything about the woman, other than what he might guess. Young, marrying perhaps for money and position. He'd known too many like that far too intimately. Instinct warned him. She might be on the make for young studs like himself. And that as exactly the kind of situation he needed to avoid.

On the other hand, she might be very much in love with her new husband and not about to screw things up with lovers on the side.

After all, women came in all shapes and sizes and designs. Some actually believed in love and marriage and loyalty. He shouldn't judge somebody he hadn't even met.

As he drove the car down the tree-lined street where his uncle lived, he shoved the thoughts about Laura Henderson away as foolish imagination. His automatic mental reflexes were making up problems that weren't even offering themselves. Laura could be nothing but his aunt! And it really wouldn't make any difference what kind of man-trap she might be. Family was family. Plus he'd have to learn to look at the future in a totally different manner than he'd learned to live in the past. With that determined thought he brought the car to a stop before a huge, lovely house.

So, he thought, *this is where Uncle Henderson hangs out! Impressive!*

Just like so many he'd enjoyed as a stud-lover with some rich woman in heat for a young house pet.

"Damn it," he cursed softly, getting out of the car. "Grow up. This is a new world. Accept it and adapt!"

CHAPTER TWO

Laura Henderson was an attractive, dark-haired woman in her early thirties. As she stood there in the large living room looking at him, Johnny Belmont had a terrible sense of uneasiness. There was no doubt about the fact that his greatest fears about her were true.

Ever since he'd been ushered into the room by the Henderson maid, Laura had merely stood there in the middle of the room, staring at him. The expression on her face was controlled; not one feature moved in response to the look in her eyes. It was her eyes which unnerved Johnny. They were filled with the wild, savage excitement of one healthy animal looking at another.

This first meeting was bluntly suggestive to his trained eye. The situation was far from the comfortable one he had expected. An icy shiver moved down his spine.

He had known beautiful women before, but Laura stunned him. She was a mixture of class and sensual excitement all rolled up into one. The expression on her face was revealingly wanton. Her lips were full and attractive, the lower large and pouty, the upper a little thinner; deep red lipstick halting at the natural line of her mouth. Her figure was trim, sensual, well proportioned, with high, nicely shaped breasts.

He could easily understand why his uncle had married her; a woman twenty years younger. But why had she married Ben? Money? She was a player, much like himself—but on the female side of the game.

"You're Johnny…" The voice was husky, but naturally so.

"Jack. I never liked that name." He stepped forward and extended his hand. The contact as they shook hands was soft, warm, and affectionate. Johnny quickly withdrew his hand. He found it hard to keep his eyes off her body. His trained mind warned that it might be difficult to keep this woman at arm's distance. He'd have to cool her, fast.

He stepped back, out of reach.

"Ben said to tell you he was terribly sorry about not being home to meet you, Jack, but he couldn't help it. He's away a lot on business. He's shooting some retakes he had no way of knowing would be necessary." Her voice was low and rich, cultured and sensual, like everything else about her. And there was that not too subtle intimate promise hidden in it; but only a trained ear would have known the ultimate meaning. She was sizing him up and mentally flirting with the idea of what might take place between them.

Their eyes met again; this time it was a pure searching exercise. No games. Immediately they recognized one another for what they were—born to be loved.

Finally Johnny hefted his small suitcase and

raised an eyebrow. "Where can I put this?"

"Oh, I'm sorry," Laura cried, rushing forward and taking hold of his shoulder. The touch was soft, electric.

Both of them froze. The look in her eyes revealed she'd felt the same electric shock. Johnny had a sudden sinking feeling. He couldn't let it happen with this woman! No matter what!

They walked down the plush hallway and up the stairs to the second floor. She directed the way into a small bedroom at the end of the hall. It had a bath and balcony and outside entrance.

"This will make your stay here a little more private. You can come and go as you please. Ben said to tell you to feel at home—raid the icebox, if that's what you want. You can do anything but bring girls up here. You do that on your own—other places." Laura's eyes covered the full length of his five-foot-eight height and finally came to rest on his face. "You're much better looking than the photos."

"What photo do you have?" Johnny asked, turning his eyes away from the woman and surveying the room.

There was a bed, large enough for three people to sleep on in comfort; it was modern and low. The dresser, on the opposite wall, was dark oak, heavy and large. There was a six-foot by three-foot mirror on the wall next to the dresser. At the side of the bed was a lamp and small night table. The other two walls were taken up by a huge closet and the balcony entrance which looked out over Beverly Hills and Los Angeles in the distance.

He heard Laura's voice murmuring in the background, but his attention was other places, other times. It was her hand on his shoulder which brought him back to the present.

The touch was far too friendly and far too pleasant. He turned, brushing her hand off his shoulder. For a moment the two of them stared at each other. She was a hot one on the make! But just as surprised and taken by the situation.

Johnny fought a flicker of raw, helpless excitement as he gazed into the woman's sensual eyes. She was supposed to be his aunt; but she was also a highly attractive woman. He had known too many like her in the past; women with money and position who didn't mind sharing the money and a bed with a handsome young stud. But Laura Henderson was his uncle's wife.

The thought depressed him, even while the images it conjured up had a strongly erotic effect on his body. He felt as if he'd been conned into a sextrap. And it was one he didn't dare play out.

"When is Ben expected back?" Johnny asked.

Her eyebrows arched. "Oh, it'll be at least three or four days."

"Oh." The implication of her casual remark was thick with open amusement. It wasn't hard to tell exactly what was she was thinking.

"You don't mind?" she inquired.

"Mind what?"

"Well—you know."

He shrugged. *Cool it, now*, he warned himself.

"Maybe I'd better leave you alone for a time. Give you a chance to get settled and unpacked and all that." She turned to leave, hesitated at the door. "If I can do anything for you—"

"Where's the booze?" Johnny started opening

his suitcase, which he'd placed on the bed.

"In the study. You'll find a little home bar. Help yourself."

"Thanks, Auntie."

"You can call me Laura. After all, there's not that much difference between our ages." She leaned against the door frame, watching him as he started unpacking his one suit, under clothing, two shirts, and jeans.

"What are you watching, Laura?" he demanded irritably, wanting her to leave. Instinct told him that open insults or blunt words would only create mocking laughter from her sensual lips. There were too people very much alike.

"You. I'm sorry. Just that I didn't know exactly what to expect. Part of the family, and all that. But I always wondered about you."

"What did you wonder?" He stuffed his shirts in the top drawer of the dresser. Purposely he refused to turn and look at Laura. He knew what was coming.

"Well, you know. Talk goes around, and—"

'I'm the black sheep in the family?" He hung his gray suit in the closet and clammed the sliding doors closed, turned and glared at the woman. No matter what, he had to make it clear to Laura how things had to be between them; once and for all.

"I didn't mean that, really, Johnny."

"Jack!"

"Okay, Jack. I didn't mean it the way it sounded. Just that Ben said you were a little wild. A hellion with the women. I didn't know what to expect, that's all." She avoided his eyes.

"Disappointed?"

"I didn't say that." She made an irritated action of her right hand, cutting the air.

"Let's drop the subject!" With that she turned and walked hurriedly down the hall.

Johnny went to the door and slowly closed it.

As he finished unpacking, Johnny kept thinking about the look in Laura's eyes as she had stormed out of the room.

She spelled trouble. No doubt she'd married for money. No woman looked at other men like that if she was happily married. A bad setup! Just the kind didn't need.

He felt the uneasy nervousness that warned him to watch out for Laura Henderson. Given the chance, she'd screw raw.

Johnny shrugged, slammed the suitcase shut, clamped the lock and tossed it into the closet. A moment later he flung himself on the bed. He decided to simply ignore any sex plays from Laura. It was the only way to survive living in the same house with her.

He lay there thinking about the young girl in the restaurant and wondering what kind of things were going on in her mind. She probably didn't like the idea of jumping for strange studs just passing through, but her little world had trapped her.

Johnny jerked his mind to the present.

"Women are bitches in heat!" he muttered softly, sitting up and studying the room.

He suddenly decided there really wasn't any danger concerning Laura as long as he simply ignored her.

This was a great layout. A real setup. Maybe things would be okay here in Hollywood. Maybe he would finally discover his place in the world. Years of bumming had worn him down to desperately seeking a resting place, a haven. He was ready to settle down to a normal, steady life. Maybe find a real woman to actually fall in love with; if that was possible.

Then he thought of Laura Henderson and the wanton looks she'd given him, and the excitement of her touch. It really didn't matter; she could hardly do more than play teasing games. Maybe she'd settle for flirtations and not try as something more intimate.

Things would work out, just as long as he kept his hands off Laura, and that he promised to do. All he needed was the woman of the house haunting his bedroom.

Sighing, Johnny stood and left the room and went downstairs. He found Laura in the living room.

She was lounging on the sofa, her legs stretched out, pillowed against the soft cushions. The skirt of her dress was high, revealing a creamy expanse of naked thigh. When she saw him, she made a quick effort to lower her skirt, but fumbled long enough to give him a good show.

"I wanted the study and booze," Johnny drawled, attempting to appear as if he hadn't noticed her leg display. He wondered how long she had lain there, waiting for him to come down for a drink.

Maybe it was an accident, he told himself. But he didn't believe it. She had taken too long to cover herself, made too much of an unnecessary display. If she hadn't wanted him to really notice, she would have either casually lowered her skirt or left it alone.

30

"Over there. Mind fixing me a drink, too?" She pointed to a doorway across the hall.

Johnny walked into the study. It was an attractive room, its walls lined with bookcases. In the middle was a huge desk, clean except for a blotter, ash tray and a cigar box covered in thick leather. A chair, with footstool and lamp, was in one corner, with a small magazine stand at its side.

All the comforts of home except the couch, Johnny thought as he stepped to the small bar opposite the reading chair.

"Where's the ice?" he called into the living room.

"Behind the bar. A small icebox. You'll find everything you need."

He walked around the bar. It was loaded with a score of bottles; everything from whiskey and rum to several expensive brandies, vermouths and liqueurs.

Helping himself to a fine, twenty-year-old scotch, he opened the small icebox which held an electric icemaker and filled two tall glasses with ice. Then he poured the scotch, stirred, found some soda water, and dropped a small amount in each glass. Then he returned to the living room.

Laura was sitting up now, her face had an expectant expression on it. There was no revelation as to what she expected, but more of an eagerness that burned in her eyes like sparkling diamonds.

As he handed her one of the drinks, Johnny studied her face, taking in the high cheekbones, the pout of lush red lips, and the wide innocent size of her eyes which belied the expression in them. She was one of those women who had complete control of most situations, except those which involved their emotions. When it came to a man, they went a little off balance, unable to keep a tight rein on their actions. He guessed that she was highly passionate once her body gained control of her mind.

Johnny sat across from her in a large, off-white chair.

He plopped his feet on the footstool in front of him and sipped the scotch.

"How'd you know I liked scotch?" Laura asked.

"A man gets to know a woman."

"Oh?" Her eyebrows arched. Interest, intrigued and commanding, flared in her eyes. "What do you know about me, or think you know?"

He gazed up at the ceiling thoughtfully. "Well, you're expensive. Take the dress you have on—bet it cost Uncle a nice piece of loot. Maybe a hundred, maybe thousand." He hesitated and then took a sip of his drink. "You're sensitive, and careful about most things—except one."

"And what do you think that is?" There was a smirk in her voice. She was too sure of herself.

He turned and looked at her. She was staring at him with a slight grin on her lips. The expression was mocking. Angrily, Johnny decided this was the time to knife her cold—but in a careful way.

"You're a passionate woman," he said, irritated, determined to break down her amusement. "Too wild for your own good!" He stood and started out of the room, saying, "So be smart and cool it!"

"Where are you going?" she asked.

The tone of her voice stopped Johnny. It was commanding.

"Out. Out for awhile."

"Wait!" Laura stood and stepped across the room toward him. The rhythm and grace of her walk was both classical and sensual. It had a respectable amount of animal appeal about it that pleased Johnny much more than he liked to admit.

"Now what, Auntie?" He tried to look bored.

"Don't put on airs with me, Jack. I know far too much about you. We're alike, you and me!"

"I guess we've managed to cut through the chill, haven't we?" Johnny announced. "Coming right to the point, aren't you?"

"And what does that mean, exactly? Spell it out, if you dare!" The smirk of amusement trembled at the corners of her lips. Her green eyes challenged him.

"We're too much alike," Johnny finally admitted in a tight, controlled voice. "Let it go there."

He started to turn, but her hand reached out to his shoulder, moving him around to face her.

"Why don't you say the rest, Jack? Tell your Aunt Laura exactly what she is!" She pressed closer; her hips were only inches from his, her lips just under his mouth. Her breasts almost touched his chest. "But watch out how you call the punches—you might just get burned."

She was staring at him seriously, expectantly. Her mouth hung open, ready for his kiss.

With a grunt of anger, Johnny pushed her away and left the room. A few moments later he found himself sitting on the patio, looking out across his uncle's large, expansive backyard.

* * * * * * *

Laura stared after her young nephew-in-law, feeling the sensations rush over her again, hungrily reaching into the very enter of that passionate heat which had driven her body for as long as she had been married.

I needed a hot stud like him, bad, she realized.

Then, as she slowly stepped back to the sofa and sat down, her mind pictured Johnny Belton as he had looked when first ushered into her living room a couple of hours before.

He had stood there, holding the worn and battered brown suitcase. His clothes were shabby, but clean enough, considering his long trip across country. Jeans and an open blue shirt. His face was lean and angular, but handsome in a boyish way. It was the kind of face that women went for instinctively. They either wanted to baby and mother him, or act like living whores. She had the intense, uncontrollable urge toward the latter. That body of his, slender compared to his uncle's heavy frame, hard as steel, invited images of the most depraved type to etch their way through her mind.

You're his aunt, she told herself, taking another sip of the scotch.

"But you're a woman, too, and unrelated, and starved for love and affection and a man. Or just raw sex!"

Laura shrugged, trying hard to be the lady that her parents and her maturity had trained her to be. It wasn't until she had met Ben Henderson that she'd learned about the driving, almost inexhaustible sexual passion that could possess her body. There had been a number of lovers before she'd met Ben Henderson, but they had been too brief, too hidden to have developed the intense, wild hunger within her. Maybe it was part of maturing, or being married to a man who couldn't fully satisfy her, Laura had argued time and time again.

But, basically, she had a wild streak that demanded feeding. And she was, quite frankly, an unrelenting flirt. One that didn't stop at mere tease. She flirted to get real thrills and followed up whenever it was possible to enjoy total intimacy with such men who responded to her. In fact, she had no trouble getting lovers.

Her mind returned to Johnny and his young, exciting body.

Johnny was the type of stud who had a raw animal appeal that made women fall quick and hard. She had heard enough about him from her husband to excite a normal interest and intrigue about his coming to live with them. A terrible inner struggle had plagued her from the first moment that Ben had announced Johnny's arrival. It was the fact that Johnny made every woman willing to fall into his arms that had excited Laura—and terrified her. If only Ben were a better lover, things might not be so difficult. Now she was trapped in the same house with a young, healthy male animal who had a reputation of knowing his way around women. They were both too sophisticated to avoid or ignore their mutual animal attractive for one another.

The look in his eyes had sent chills down Laura's spine. It had taken all the control she had to keep from stripping naked right from the first moment.

She gulped the rest of the scotch and went into the study for some more.

You drink too much, she warned herself, too much....

Stepping to the window, she looked out onto the patio where Johnny was sitting. Her eyes feasted on the youthful strength of his lean body, and that tingling sensation drove through her.

Suddenly she wanted to scream, to run, and to find escape from the sudden impossible situation. The idea of carrying on with Johnny was all too tempting. How easy for them to enjoy long intimate moments together whenever Ben wasn't home—and he wasn't very often. But that could be a dangerous game. A very excitingly dangerous game.

Why couldn't Ben have been here, her mind sobbed. *Why?*

Every nerve in her body screamed out to have Johnny touch her.

But that wasn't new either, she realized. She'd always been man-hungry.

In the last six months, with Ben away most of the time, Laura had been driven wild. Then one night she had found herself in a bar, talking to a strange, handsome man. They had left and gone to a motel.

Since then there had been a lot of nights like that one.

Each had its special kick. It seemed better each time.

It happened once or twice a month now. She couldn't stand the craving of her body, the nerves that grew raw with wanting.

Ben wasn't able to satisfy her needs—pickups did.

CHAPTER THREE

As Johnny sat out on the patio, his thoughts turned back the years, an inner anguish peeling the pages of his life as though he were reading a book. A Mardi Gras of impressions, smells, sensations, fears; and war. *The War of Johnny Belton Against the World.*

His mother had been a real bum; his father had divorced her when Johnny was merely a kid. He didn't really remember his mother. From what he'd heard about her, she was a tramp, a no-good who sank lower and lower. Her brother, Ben Henderson, had done everything he could to help her through the last years of her life.

It wasn't until after her death five years back, when he was twenty-two, that Johnny had heard any word from Ben Henderson.

The day he'd received the letter that told of his mother's death, Johnny was lying in a small, flea-bitten shack with a little baby-faced bar slut he'd picked up the night before. A hangover was bounding from one side of his head to the other. The woman had played the sex game from every possible position and angle; she had known a few tricks that even his experience had missed. They had drunk most of the night and picked the drinking up in the morning to wash away their hangovers. And then they started in again on each other's bodies.

At one point, after he'd left her to fix drinks and returned to the bed, she was sitting on the edge of it, legs parted wide in open erotic offer.

"Let me play with it first!" she suggested huskily.

They were just about to embrace when a heavy pounding sounded on the door.

Both of them froze. The girl's face had twisted into a pleading. "No, don't answer it." Her hands gripped his groin, urging it toward her thighs.

Forcefully he disengaged himself from her and called: "What is it?"

A voice came through the door panel: "Letter. Special Delivery from California—Hollywood," came the friendly voice of the mailman.

With a grunt of irritation, Johnny had pushed the woman away and went to the door, opened it a crack.

Johnny waited until the letter was put in his hand, then he closed the door. He ripped open the envelope and then spread out the sheet of typewritten paper, reading:

"Dear John,

"Your mother passed away last Friday. I know that doesn't mean a lot to you, for you hardly knew her. My sister was a lonely, tormented woman, and when your father took you away from her she went rock bottom and

never recovered. But she didn't forget you. I'm sending a couple of thousand dollars to you—that's the amount in her personal account. Legal difficulties will keep the money tied up, but I'm handling everything for her. She wanted you to have the money as soon as possible. I hope you'll accept it in her name. And if you ever need anything, don't hesitate to contact me.

"Your Uncle Ben."

The money had come a couple of days later, but he'd kept himself in a high state of drunkenness and kept the woman around to entertain him until he had the money to get out of the town. He had been trapped there for six months, trying to make ends meet. The shack was his father's, and when Johnny had come back from Korea he'd gone there to live, having no other place to stay.

The money from Henderson started him out on a long spree around the country. It gave him the start to go to Kansas City, where he worked as a ditch digger, salesman, and dishwasher. From town to town, from job to job he'd wandered, and then caught onto the cushy, easy life when he'd been in a swank bar one night in a small town in the middle of Georgia. There he met a young woman who acted and looked like at least twenty-two, but turned out to be well under age. He picked her up and took her to a motel.

But the way she acted, pulling off her sweater immediately upon entering the room, releasing her tight bra to reveal full, plump young breasts and lovely virgin nipples, he knew she was a little tramp, highly skilled in sex.

They spent the night screwing like mad. The morning had brought her father, a rich landowner— and the law. The two of them were married a few hours later. Her father didn't seem to be at all inter- esting in his lack of social skills or lack of back- ground. It was that or jail. It was a rather cut and dried "shot gun" marriage. The girl was delighted to have a built in stud living with her. Only later he learned that the family was glad to get her hooked up with any male, hoping that might settle her down, at least for a while. He'd actually believed it might work out. She'd been hot sexually—and was very rich. The next year had been both agonizing and instructive.

He had lived with his young bride in a large southern house with her father and mother. The so- cial life the family lived had taught him enough to learn his way around any society dame. The bride wouldn't leave him alone sexually. It turned out that she was over-sexed and was even too much for him. When he found her in bed with a couple of local guys, it hadn't been difficult to get a divorce and nice settlement.

After that Johnny had again spread it around the country, but this time in style. By the time his money had run out, he was attending to the charms of a woman in her early forties who had enough cash to keep him around until she tired of his com- pany. After that he'd bummed from place to place until he'd met up with Carol Laymont. It was a business arrangement. She wanted his body; he enjoyed her money. But the relationship was getting a bit strained after eight months. He'd stayed with her until he'd finally received his uncle's invitation to come out west and go to work for him. "There's plenty of opportunity out here, and if you're really interested I can see to it that you're given the chance to make good. It's the least I can do for my sister's son," had been his uncle's final offer.

Johnny brought his mind back to the present. He lighted a cigarette.

He thought about Laura Henderson, realizing it was going to be difficult to ignore her sexual charms and subtle offers. If he stayed very long in this house they would end up together in some bed—unless he could cool things right at the beginning.

Fat chance.

That evening at dinner, Laura was silent and distant. She only conversed with Johnny when it was necessary. They ate their pot roast, mashed potatoes and candied yams in utter silence. During coffee he tried to break through the stilted atmosphere. The only response that he received from Laura was quick answers and silence. Her eyes were the only things alive and active during the meal and coffee; they kept studying him like some delicious object that she would like to feed upon. After dinner Johnny went for a walk, down along the curving road that led to the Henderson home. The house was in Beverly Hills, overlooking the famous "Hollywood star" section of Los Angeles. It was late when he finally returned to the house. He went up to his room through the private entrance of the balcony. As he was climbing into bed, he heard footsteps in the hallway; they stopped in front of his door.

Johnny tensed It could be nobody other than Laura. It was some time before she walked away. Johnny lay there in the darkness thinking about what would have happened if Laura had walked into his room.

His imagination filled in long details, hours of caressing her body, of kissing her soft, white flesh. The temptation was unnerving. With any other woman there would have been no questions asked. Sex and more sex.

Finally sleep clouded his mind, but dreams haunted his rest. Most of the dreams concerned Laura, or some faceless woman who kept chasing him through the large house. When he woke up the next morning, his body was drenched in sweat.

The day was another study in silent torment. Neither Laura nor Johnny made any effort at conversation. But when they found each other in the same room, there was a heavy electric thickness to the air. When their eyes met, it was as if their minds had connected. Each silently was saying the same thing: how long could they hold out.

Johnny spent the afternoon in the backyard near the swimming pool. Later, in the evening, he drove into Hollywood, taking in the famous sites. The corner of Hollywood and Vine was the great disappointment that he had almost half expected it to be. Everything that civilization labeled as glamorous usually turned out to be all words with nothing behind it. The corner was like all other corners in the world. He parked his car and walked down Hollywood Boulevard, reading the names of the stars that had been set into the sidewalk. There were a few dollars in his wallet, left from his trip, and he stepped into a cocktail lounge and had several drinks, then returned to his car. An hour later he was walking into the Henderson home.

Laura was in the living room watching television. As he passed the doorway, she called to him.

Laura was sitting on the sofa, her legs stretched out on a footstool. In her right hand was a tall glass. She was dressed in slacks and white blouse. The blouse was open at the top and he could just make out the edge of her bra. She looked loaded.

But the very sensual sight of this beautiful woman created a quick rushing of his blood that flashed heat into every nerve. Already he felt that his pants had become too small, too confining.

"Where you been?" she asked, her eyes stripping his body.

"Out. Just out and around, seeing the sights of the great movie capital!" He leaned against the doorway, his eyes turning to the TV set. An old English movie was playing.

"I'm sorry about the other day." Her voice was sultry.

"So—so am I—but where does that leave us?" Damned his blasted hard.

She shrugged, then said: "Why don't you help yourself to a drink and join me?"

He hesitated. Instinctively he knew just how easy it would be to snap her right into bed. Just like that. On the other than, the situation had to be resolved. He considered the options and then decided there wasn't any reason not to accept her awkward attempt to mend their relationship. If they were to live together in the same house, they might as well try to get along. And it had to start sooner or later. Sooner the better. Maybe she'd realized how impossible the situation was. They could hardly try any-thing too personal or intimate. Maybe she simply wanted to be friendly.

In moments he had fixed himself a scotch and soda and stepped into the living room.

Laura patted the sofa and said, "Over here."

Johnny hesitated and then walked over and sat down near her. His nerves were alert, ready to fight back any advance. This was, perhaps, he realized, an attempt on both of their parts to learn how to ac-cept each other—as relatives, and not as anything else.

The game had to be played out, one way or an-other. There was no coy way around it.

Johnny tried to keep his attention on the televi-sion set. But the movie was boring, and his eyes kept drifting to the woman next to him. The situa-tion was impossible. His pants felt painfully tight.

Her legs were wonderful under the tight fit of her slacks. Her breasts jutted tauntingly against the white of the blouse. He gulped at the hot knot in his throat.

Suddenly Laura turned and looked at him. Her eyes were glazed from liquor, her expression bold and brazen. For a moment she studied him and then smiled.

"I guess we started out badly."

"Yes, I suppose so."

"We're human, so..."

"Yes...but there has to be a line drawn. We both know it," he simply said, trying hard to avoid look-ing at her lovely body.

"Sure. I guess so. Of course you're right. I know it. You know it. But...oh, Jack...I know how wrong

44

it is, but I almost wish you hadn't come here "

She looked away.

"I can leave," Johnny offered.

"No! Ben wouldn't allow it. He'd never forgive me. We just have to learn to live with it." She refused to face him as they talked. Her eyes were fastened on the television set.

Johnny wanted to tell her so many things. They had no business being attracted to one another. He wanted to somehow give her strength, to help her. And most of all bring things out in the open, unemotionally—so they could agree to keep things cooled, come to an honest agreement.

It was so painfully obvious that both of them were hot for one another; both were basically carnal animals, alone in a large house, and needy at hell.

"Jack, we have to find some way to get along. Without...this...thing...between us."

"I know." *So*, he thought, *maybe she was trying to settle the obviously painful issue.*

"I mean, Jack," she turned, looked at him, "somehow so that we aren't tormented like... damned fact is you turn me on. We both know it. And you're just as hot for me. We're like two jungle animals in heat, circling one another, sizing one another up and getting ready for the kill. We're both hot for one another in a big way!"

"Stop it! Just stop it, Laura. So, we are a lot alike. I suppose. And, frankly, you *are* really something! But...as they say, no way, José! To put it bluntly, right on the line: we'd both be damned fools to play in that sandbox. Best to keep it cooled. At a distance. After Ben returns, I'll find some way to move out, get an apartment of my own. I can't live off you folks. And the temptation will be cut out of our lives. Does that make sense?"

Silence. Then, "I never met a man like you. Maybe your reputation. No. That's crap! Some people meet and fire sparks. And—"

"That's the trouble. We're too much alike." Johnny stood. "So we agree to the terms? Hands off!"

He started for the hallway.

He was physically shaken. The erection still pressed painfully against his pants.

"Jack, please!" she cried. "Don't leave me."

He turned, startled by her words.

Her eyes feasted on him, like a hungry beast, desperately needy. It was obvious she'd been drinking a bit too much. For a lingering moment it almost appeared she would just stand there, staring longingly at him. Then, without warning, almost impulsively, Laura rushed toward him. She simply her arms around his neck.

"No!" Johnny cried, attempting to push the woman away. "No!"

But Laura's lips were already too close. Her thigh surged forcefully between his thighs.

The kiss was like soft, electric fire that surged a fury of desire throughout his body. The softness of her form as it hugged against his was overpowering. Her lips sucked violently on his tongue. He couldn't resist the embrace any more than he could stop breathing.

Finally they broke apart, panting, staring in torment into each other's eyes.

"Let's forget that, Laura. You were a little high and—"

"No! No, Johnny. You don't know how it is to live in…. Oh God, what am I saying?" She violently shook her head from side to side. "Oh, God—what have I done?"

She rushed out of the room and up the stairs.

Johnny stood there for a little while and then went to the second floor and into his room, still feeling the throbbing pain of a tight knotted-up hard against his pants.

He heard Laura's soft crying from across the hallway, where her room was located. It continued for a long time. He smoked a lot, and looked out over the expanse of Los Angeles through the balcony windows.

Finally he undressed and went to bed.

Now, for the first time, Johnny knew for certain that there was something drastically wrong with his uncle's marriage with Laura. And whatever it was was slowly driving Laura to some emotional breakdown. Also, he realized that she apparently loved her husband. It might not have been so difficult if this wasn't so obvious.

How he'd love to ravish her lush body! There was no question about his own attraction to her. But he'd felt that way about a lot of women. And, in the past, had made it right into their beds. No guilt. He was in the habit of taking what he wanted when he could have it. With Laura it would simply be a matter of opening his arms to her.

He was aware of footsteps moving across the hall. Then the door of his room opened, a crack. Johnny froze, closing his eyes.

"Jack—are you awake?"

He didn't move, hardly breathing for fear of

saying or doing the wrong thing.

"Jack, please, if you're awake, will you—?" The door snapped shut.

Johnny waited, almost afraid that she had entered the room. Then he heard her move across the hallway and then close her bedroom door.

Johnny sighed and relaxed. Too close. If she'd come in, nothing would have stopped them from relieving their hot need.

It was some time before sleep finally settled over his mind and body—before the hardness of his groin relaxed and made it possible to sleep.

* * * * * * *

Laura sat on the bed, digging her hand into her thighs until the pain numbed some of the mental torment.

How close it had been! It was the drinks, she told herself, knowing what a lie that was. Drunk or sober, soon something was going to happen. The long nights, alone, with Johnny across the hall from her, would drain her resistance, her strength. The mere thought of him so close excited her body beyond her ability to control them:

That kiss had paralyzed her mind. Her body burned!

Why, why had she let it happen? her mind screamed. But the answer was all too simple.

Lying back on the bed, she tried to close out her thoughts, tried to calm the ragged nerves.

Somehow she had to get Johnny off her mind.

The feel of his body had wired her desire like a hard knot throughout her whole body. She knew he wanted her, too, in a big way. It was written in his eyes every time he looked at her. Ever since that first moment when their eyes had met, they had both felt the irresistible pull, the wild, insane desire. Both of them knew it, and were aware that the other knew it.

And every time he looked at her she could feel his hot desire. It was like being physically touched, caressed by his eyes in a very erotic way. Her body responded almost electrically.

Maybe, she thought, sitting up and reaching for a cigarette, a party would help—a girl to get his mind off her.

At least that would be a start. They had to mend a cushioned distance between them, had to keep a wall locked into place.

What was so frightening was the fact of how easy it would be to be with Johnny—just slipping into his bed would be all it might take. Seducing him would not even a question but merely a natural act of two people submitting to their mutual desire.

He needed to be offered up some other object to feast his animal attentions on. That would be the beginning of building a healthy wall between them.

Jealousy stabbed through Laura at the thought of setting Johnny up with another girl. But the idea intrigued her, too. It was a desperate, wild scheme, but maybe the only logical one. If he just wouldn't look at her the way he did, if he had another woman to keep him active, maybe things would be easier for her.

Then her mind clicked onto a plan. Jean Harold might be just the trick. Jean and her latest party-film Ben had produced. Jean was a hot young female, and probably would offer no resistance to Johnny's charms. He was a man who knew exactly how to seduce a woman with his eyes; and he read a woman like a book. He could make her feel naked right down to the bones.

Jean would hardly object to being with Johnny. And he'd certainly find her attractive.

With his sensual attention diverted, it would be easier for her to deal with the situation.

Laura lay on the bed for a long time.

Yes, she thought frantically, get his attention involved with another woman and it might possibly take the edge off so that they would live out the next days until Ben returned. After that, things would be easier. They couldn't get worse.

She hoped it would work. But she knew the terrible ache it would give her to think of him with another woman.

And that, she realized, was ridiculous.

* * * * * * *

The next day Johnny had been swimming, taking in the hot California sunshine, when Laura's voice called him into the house. He pulled himself out of the pool and quickly dried his body.

He found Laura in the living room, talking on the phone.

She broke off when he entered.

"Oh, Jack, there's going to be a small party here tonight. Nothing big, but I was wondering if you have anything to wear."

"A suit, not pressed."

"I can arrange to have a girl come along for you.

I'm speaking to Ben's partner. He knows a lot of girls..." The look in her eyes flared for a moment, then softened. She covered the mouthpiece and hissed softly over it to him. "I'm sorry about what happened last night."

"Forget it, Laura." Johnny shrugged. "It just happened."

"It was a mistake, wasn't it?" she whispered. Her eyes looked frightened. "It won't happen again?"

The meaning was obvious.

"What is this—a question and answer game? Forget it! Get some broad to keep me company, and—no! To hell with it. I don't feel like blasting out tonight. I'll take a ride."

"No need to do that. Larry would be glad to get you a swinging girl. There's only going to be him and another two couples. Hollywood people. They're interesting. I think you'd enjoy yourself. You might learn something about Hollywood." There was a silent implication to her last words, but the meaning was lost to him. "Good connections."

Johnny hesitated, then shrugged. "Why not? Tell him to bring something like Liz—"

'Don't be silly!' Laura snapped. Then into the receiver she said: "Oh, wait, Larry—I'll be right with you!" She turned her eyes back to Johnny. "Look, I can't hold on forever."

There was an odd look on her face; an excitement that was so intense that Johnny could feel it reach out and caress him. "Please! I promise you, you'll have a ball!"

"Okay—have him send over some nice lady."

"That I promise!" she stated.

Johnny walked across the hall and into the study. A minute later he returned to the living room with a stiff drink of straight scotch. He sipped the liquor as he watched Laura talk to Larry.

The sight of her created an immediate sensual reaction. She was posed in such a way that the thrust of her breasts and the circling, rounded flare of hips were accented to his view. The body interest was captivating.

The woman was a natural flirt, a female who simply moved automatically into sensual positions, who simply couldn't avoid showing herself off in a manner that blatantly invited a man's eyes.

Finally she hung up and turned toward him.

"He's bringing Jean Harold over. A lovely little girl. Just your age—I'm afraid you'll like her." The gleam in her eyes was greener than usual. They were automatically stripped his lean body. After a moment she sighed. "Sometimes I wish things were different."

She walked out of the room, and as she passed him the light smell of sensual perfume filled the air. It was all he needed.

Johnny stood there for a long time, until he had finished the scotch. Then he went into the study, mixed himself another drink, and went over to the reading chair in the corner and plunked down into it.

There was a book on the magazine stand— Henry Miller's *Tropic of Cancer*.

Johnny thumbed through it, picking up the four-letter words and the interesting parts, then he got bored and slammed it down on the rack again.

Maybe it was a mistake coming to Hollywood, he told himself irritably. Or maybe he should have waited a few more days? But how was he to have known that Ben Henderson wouldn't be there when he arrived. Or that his wife was a hot chick who was furiously needy—and all too available.

Something annoyed him about the party that was planned for the evening. There had been a certain light in Laura's eyes when she'd said he might learn something about Hollywood; the tone of her voice had implied something other than the normal information of behind-the-scenes gossip about the movie industry.

He wondered about the Jean Harold who was coming to even the couples out. Would she turn out to be a seductive offering? He almost figured that Laura was setting him up for a distraction. At least she was trying to make things easier for the two of them..

As he left the study to go up to his room, there was an uneasy feeling gnawing at the lining of his stomach.

Getting undressed, he went info the small half-bath, moved into the shower stall and turned on the cold water.

By the time he had dressed in his gray suit, Johnny was feeling a little better, and even looking forward to meeting his blind date, Jean Harold. Laura had promised him a good-time woman. And that could mean only one thing, considering how much she surely realized he needed one.

Johnny understood Laura enough to pretty much read her mind on this matter. She was setting him up with something to distract his attention. Smart play.

CHAPTER FOUR

Right from the instant he saw Jean Harold, Johnny was taken by a wild surge of immediate desire and interest. She was a soft, willowy girl, closer to twenty than she was to thirty, and lovely, deliciously attractive and amazingly warm. Her long, blonde hair flowed over her shoulder like silken wavy arms. She had long, tapered fingers that ended in red nails, pointed and dangerous looking. Her blue eyes were soft, bold, and experienced. The full, nicely shaped red lips were seductively inviting. On introduction she'd simply stepped forward, and without embarrassment, had given him a very warm hug. For just an instant it felt as if she would have kissed him, but her lips lingered only a moment as she stepped back.

Johnny didn't even get a chance to really take the woman's image in detail. She was a flash of color, sensual beauty and movement. There were others who came into the room along with her. Things moved swiftly after that.

Almost immediately the two of them had gone to get drinks in the study.

"Been in Hollywood long?" she asked, conversationally.

"Just a few days," he said, stepping around the bar. "What do you drink?"

"Nothing too strong. I had a couple before getting here."

"Oh. Need it to face a blind date?"

"Well blind date is one thing...but I don't want to be blind drunk!" she laughed, very unaffectedly. "Just a highball."

"Is that a suggestive remark!" he teased, feeling suddenly very comfortable with her.

"Only if that's okay with you," she swiftly countered, winking. "But I wouldn't want you to be shocked, of course!"

"Of course," he chuckled, mixing the drinks.

She watched him fixing the drinks, and he felt a flush of warmth rush through him under her even, level gaze.

"Like what you see?" he offered, not glancing up at her.

"Nice. Do you like me?"

He didn't move, silence surrounded him. He looked up and found her eyes gazing directly into his. There was intimate warmth there, and something else that was quite nice. He wondered what. Why was he so off balance with Jean?

"I...think you're...cute," he offered, handing over the highball.

"Is that all? Just cute?" She pouted, appearing almost hurt.

"Okay. What would you like me to say?"

"Well, a girl likes to think her man...well...her date...thinks she's kinda...well, you know."

"Attractive?"

"Why not?"

He simply let his eyes flow over her body, hesitating for a long obvious moment on her breasts which were so nicely displayed.

"Well, Jack, I think that says it all!" she laughed throatily as their eyes met again. "I must thank you most…well, thankfully."

As he came around the bar she moved close and the two of them were suddenly touching. It happened so swiftly that he didn't really have a chance to do more than react.

Their lips met, parted, hungrily. Their bodies arched against one another. It was fast, and immediate. Hot and intimate. And strangely so natural. Without so much as a pause they parted, and their hands met, fingers intertwining.

Neither of them said a word as they left the room and joined the others. But they continued holding hands and her fingers in his were warm, sensual, promising.

Jean clung close to him in a warm, friendly manner, as if they had been socially friendly for a long.

The general conversation was about nothing. It was cocktail time and the party was warming rapidly. Larry Jenkins was setting up a projector for the film that he'd brought over. Laura had watched him with a look in her eyes that was far from impersonal.

Jimmy Dale and his young wife made up one couple; Johnny had forgotten about the other two the minute they were introduced to him. Both couples paid more attention to each other's mates than their own.

It was all happening so fast that he didn't get a

chance to do more than react. The others seemed to know one another in a very intimate way and were not playing any games concerning that fact. They interacted automatically. It was as if they were playing out a scripted scene.

"Might as well get down to business!" somebody said. "Pick your place to sit…and enjoy!"

Johnny sat on the sofa with Jean, who leaned close, her thigh touching his. He instinctively placed an arm around her. It was all natural, unaffected. They both seemed to feel comfortable with one another, like old friends. It was almost startlingly intimate and warm.

She leaned against him in such a way that her firm, youthful breast pressed into his chest. She was a lovely young woman, and he imagined that before she'd hit Hollywood she'd been quite nice and a little innocent. Now she was unafraid to show her willingness to be a woman, nor her willingness to share beds with a right guy.

"I like you," she murmured softly, almost intimately. "Better than I expected."

"Oh?"

"Sure. You weren't handed over to me without some background."

"Oh? Now you have me curious."

"Don't be. I was told to expect a charmingly attractive young man. To dress to the hilt. And that I'd probably like you."

"Now…you're teasing me."

"Not at all. But that might be fun!" she giggled lightly at that.

"Are you flirting again?" he chuckled.

"Would you like that?"

"Depends."

"On what?" She leaned closer, her cheek almost brushing his. She whispered in his ear: "How'd you like me to flirt with you, Jack?"

"Without any holds barred, maybe."

"Maybe that might be nice. We'll see." But her lips touched his neck, just barely. "I think you're nice."

Then she pulled away.

"More drinks?" Laura's voice asked.

"Sure. More drinks! All around!"

The two of them simply sat there, aware of one another, as drinks were brought to them.

She smiled while sipping her highball.

He was aware of the warmth of her thigh against his. He was also aware of the intimacy of the whole room. There was a very raw atmosphere of sensuality lingering all around them; unspoken, but very alive. It was more like a kind of expectation, everybody waiting for the right moment to let the sparks fly.

Johnny was somewhat puzzled. He felt in some ways kind of uncomfortable. He wanted to get away from the others, alone with Jean.

"What'd you come to Hollywood for, Jack?" Jean's soft, low voice inquired. It was enough to give any man an erection. She moved her head to look up at him. The ripe velvet of her lips was only inches from his. He lowered his head to kiss her. The point of her tongue surged out and caressed the surface of his lips, then she withdrew, shaking her head. "I didn't ask you to kiss me. I asked—"

"Why I'd come to Hollywood." He let his hand slide further around her body so that the fingers pressed the curve of her breast. The flesh was soft, supple.

She didn't seem to notice.

"Here to get in pictures?"

"Nothing like that. Just to make a place for myself," he assured her, finding it almost impossible to drag her into his arms for a deeply passionate embrace.

"You could make it in films—if you can act. You have the raw animal charm about you that would go over big with the women. But I guess you already know that!"

He smiled but said nothing.

His mind wandered for a little while, remembering when the two of them had been alone in the study.

Her voice jarred him out of the memory. "You aren't listening to me."

"I'm sorry. I was thinking about you, though."

"What?" Her voice was tense with intrigue.

"That kiss."

She laughed throatily and turned her eyes away from him.

"What kind of movie is this Larry Jenkins going to show us?"

Jean's face lighted and she squeezed his thigh lightly with delicate fingers. "The kind they don't show in theaters."

Johnny felt a gripping claw at his stomach. He turned and looked around the room. A sex film was all he needed.

Laura was sitting very close to Larry Jenkins, whispering, holding a glass between her hands. The heavy-set man glanced up and looked at Johnny. He grinned and nodded.

Johnny looked away. The other two couples were completely occupied by each other's partners.

He turned his attention back to Jean. "What kind of people are you, anyway?"

"Why?" She frowned.

"Don't you know anything about the respectability of marriage?" He nodded to the married couples who had changed partners. He felt foolish having said that. After all, he'd been around swingers before; many times. Yet for some reason he felt a need to appear somewhat oblivious to that kind of life style. Why? He wondered. Games. Just games. Always nasty little games.

She merely laughed, then said: "You'll find out a lot of things about this town and what it does to people. I came here with stars in my eyes—three years ago, via the beauty contests. And boy, were those stars put out, but fast. The first real-life chance I got for a real-live part in a movie was in the form of a blatant proposition; come to bed with me and you get the part."

"I didn't think they were that crude about it," Johnny admitted. He felt suddenly sorry for Jean. She looked like such a nice, decent girl.

"You'd be surprised, Jack. They are real bastards. And believe me, if they don't get you into bed, you don't get the part—unless you have some other pull..."

"I should think you'd get pretty tired of that kind of man—even get to hate them!" Johnny observed, studying her innocent-looking face.

She grinned and shook her head. "It depends on the man. Those movie slobs are part of the business—you either fight them or join them. Social life is something different."

"And you're just a little girl on a date, then?" Johnny offered, squeezing her closer to him. He felt a sudden tenderness for her, and couldn't understand why. It didn't make sense.

"Something like that," she murmured in a very small voice.

Larry Jenkins stood and announced that the projector was fed and ready to produce. "Somebody turn out the lights."

Johnny felt a thread of excitement eat its way through him. The nearness of the girl in his arms, the drinks, and now the promise of a suggestive or downright sexy film were having their effects on him. His pants were too damned tight already. He'd never actually seen a stag movie. Had never found it necessary. He didn't know how it would affect him.

The lights flicked out one by one and then the projector was turned on. The murmuring of the motor was the only sound in the quiet room.

A frame of bright light flickered on the far wall.

Then a scene of a country meadow burst into existence. A title faded in, *Love in the Country*, and then quickly faded out.

Jean tensed against him. Her leg pressed closer to his. The soft pressure of her thigh was more exciting than the prospects of what was going to happen on the film.

A suggestion of doubt ate at his mind. He didn't know how he would like what was probably going to follow.

The picture panned and showed a dirt road with a couple walking down it, the man carrying a blan-

ket and lunch basket.

They walked over to a large tree off the road and sat down next to each other. They kissed lightly and the man tried to play his hands into the woman's breasts. She laughed and brushed his hands away. There wasn't any sound track, but it was obvious that she had said "Later."

They unpacked the lunch. The camera got a full view of the low neckline of the woman's blouse, revealing two nicely formed breasts. They talked and laughed and ate, drank beer, and looked at each other in that intimate way of lovers.

Up to this point, Johnny had been too involved in concerns about his reaction to the film. He hadn't really noticed the woman on the screen. When he did, an alarm ground his stomach into steel. The woman was Jean Harold.

Instinctively his arm slipped away from Jean. Then, realizing what he'd done, he replaced it, but not holding her quite so closely.

The sudden shock of realization had numbed his senses.

"I didn't know you were—"

"I thought you knew," she said. There was an edge of alarm in her voice. She pulled away, as if instinctively guessing at his reaction.

For a moment he didn't do anything. He was fighting a mental battle against his own normal discomfort at what was happening. Then he shrugged and pulled Jean closer, snuggling her breast with his hand. Gently she dropped her hand to his thigh; intimate, but not crude—just resting there in soft warmth.

He returned his attention to the screen.

The girl in the film stood, pulled off her blouse, and then unclasped her bra. The breasts were beautifully shaped, the under curve moving gracefully up to the rosy points.

Johnny felt a sharp physical reaction at seeing Jean's naked body on the screen, while his hand was pressed against her breast.

God, he was hard.

The Jean on the screen quickly stepped out of her skirt and then pulled off her panties. She stood over the man, happily grinning down at his now naked body. Her hand reached playfully for his limp penis and then darted teasingly around it, then withdrew. He reached for her and yanked her down beside him.

Johnny suddenly realized that he was tense, rigid, and feeling like a damned fool. A thin nausea ached at the pit of his stomach. For a moment longer he sat there, his eyes paralyzed to the screen, watching the foreplay of the screen lovers as they caressed one another. Then suddenly he simply stood and moved across the room, passing through the thin projection of light.

He wasn't shocked in a moral sense, but merely annoyed and disinterested. And angry. He needed a drink and a moment to think; to resolve his reactions; understand them.

Most of all he wanted to take Jean and literally devour her in a carnal act that would make the film they playing seem like a child's cartoon. It was a natural, normal reaction. Yet for some reason he felt cheap, almost turned off by the whole scene.

It was more the unexpected surprise of seeing Jean's body naked on the screen and playing out sexual acts which any man might want to enjoy with her. And what he wanted to experience. He knew that much.

As to the stag film; he'd known worse things. That was another matter completely.

Johnny fought the quick anger that ate at his guts.

"What's wrong, Jack?" Laura's voice taunted, mockingly. "Too hot for you?"

Johnny went into the study and slammed the door behind him. He moved to the bar and poured himself a stiff jolt of raw whiskey that he downed in three large swallows. His hands were shaking. The liquor took several long agonizing moments to take any effect.

He cursed softly to himself, slamming the empty glass on the bar. His own violent reaction shocked him.

The study door opened and Jean Harold stepped timidly in. She closed the door and then leaned back against it, studying Johnny.

After a moment she said in a small voice, "I was sure that Laura would have told you. I'm sorry. We must seem pretty weird and...well...shocking! A nasty trick, not telling you." She glided gracefully across the room toward him. At the bar she poured herself a glass of whiskey, topped it with soda water, and then took a strong swallow. "It's not as terrible as you think, Jack."

"Does it give you a cheap thrill?" he demanded nastily. He refilled his glass and gazed down at it. "You dig making that kind of film?"

Her voice was shaking as she answered him. "No! I don't."

64

"1 was beginning to actually like you. Feel sorry for you. But—" Johnny laughed. It was a bitter sound, biting, rasping.

"Now you don't?" she asked in almost a whisper.

"Now I think you're just a…well you fill in the blanks!" He was about to say more, but Jean's hand slapped out like a sledge against his right cheek.

"What did you expect? Snow White? Where do you come off?"

Stunned, Johnny clamped his fingers around her wrist, squeezing as hard as he could. "Don't you ever do a thing like that again!"

"You're hurting me!" she retorted. "And don't play the moral prude. I was told you used women! A kept man. A male stud for hire! We all do what we have to…"

"Crap!" His hand opened, releasing her wrist, realizing she had no more than pointed out the truth about him. And at the same time elevated her film to a different level; not much different from his own past acts to survive.

Johnny gulped on the whiskey. The liquor was beginning to burn his brain like fire. He looked at Jean and saw her image as it was on the screen.

"I thought it was a shit," he choked out, pressing the glass onto the bar. His knuckles were white. "I've done some pretty shabby things, I suppose. Though not in public! But that—what'd it feel like?"

For a long time silence filled the room. When Jean finally spoke, her voice was soft, controlled. "I didn't feel a thing. And I don't know why I bother even explaining to you. But, if you must know, a girl makes her way as best she can. And you shouldn't look so shocked—your dear sweet uncle was the man who got me into this racket, and he's the one who produced the picture—and many more like it!"

With that she turned and started out of the room. "He's not a very nice bastard!"

"Wait!" Johnny called, rushing after her. He whipped Jean around by the shoulders and suddenly crushed her against him. It was a strangely tender, protective act, totally different from what he had expected. He merely held her close, cradling her head against his chest. For a long time they stood somewhat stiffly against one another, then he cupped her face in his hands, looking down into those haunting eyes. He couldn't read her reaction to him or the embrace. Suddenly he was feeling emotions that were overwhelming.

Suddenly their lips met, but she was stonily unresponsive. He tried to work his tongue past her lips, but her mouth was tightly closed. With a curse, Johnny pushed her away.

She glared at him, red flushing her cheeks, her blue eyes were now hard as ice. "Regardless of what you might think about me, I'm not the type of girl who jumps into bed with every rooster that waves at me! And...and if...if you think it's been..."

Tears started down her cheeks and she turned, covering her face with delicate hands. She stood there, her back shaking in response to the soft sobs that came from her lips.

Johnny stood there, stunned. He took several deep breaths, trying to control the sudden emotional wave that had broken over him.

"I'm sorry," he managed, not even knowing why he was sorry. Looking at Jean Harold standing there sobbing, he felt as agonized as she, but for different reasons.

This was the first girl he had ever known that puzzled him. He was sure he'd had her pegged pretty good right from the beginning; now he couldn't guess at what motivated her.

Tenderly he reached out an arm and touched her shoulder.

"Leave me alone!" she snapped, turning and wiping her eyes. It was some time before she gained control over herself. "I hate that half of myself," she announced, pointing toward the living room. "I hate it! I didn't come to Hollywood to do that kind of thing. It happened—you talk to your damned uncle about that—he can tell you all about the dirty little racket he's in. He'll open your eyes, little boy! Then you'll have a right to start poking your mouth into other people's business. You don't have the right to judge me—or anybody!"

Johnny tensed at her last remark. Then he shrugged. "Look, so I'm new at this whole thing. I'm sorry. I said I'm sorry. Can we start all over again?"

"No—not right now. Never, maybe." Then she looked puzzled. "Why?"

Johnny started to say something, but his mouth hung open, with no sound coming out.

Why did he want to bother? Why was she trying to explain to him? It didn't make sense because they were complete strangers, and had no reason to even be troubled with each other's opinions.

One a kept male stud; the other a porn star.

"I don't know," he finally mumbled, suddenly embarrassed. He felt like a tiny boy who had never known the intimacy of a woman. He stared at her as if he'd never seen a woman before.

She said, "I don't know why I came in here. But I felt sorry for you—and ashamed at myself, Jack. It's all very silly and childish. You're nothing to me. I'm nothing to you. But I still want you to understand. I don't want to look cheap and dirty to you— or anybody. I know it sounds silly, but I guess you're the first guy I've been with to a party like this that didn't know about me, that was an outsider who didn't know about us—about all of us! I...I..." Her voice went dead, the tears started welling in her eyes.

"You can just go to hell!" she cried, rushing out of the room and slamming the door after her.

Johnny stood there for a moment and then turned his attention to the drink on the bar. He finished it off, refilled the glass, went over to the chair in the corner and sat down thoughtfully.

He was inwardly shaking and didn't know why. The wanting that burst through him, mixed with an inner disgust at the films, plus realizing that a woman like Jean—so beautiful and desirable, clean and pure looking—would make such a picture, made him sickly disgusted with the whole thing.

He furiously swallowed the drink, trying to force his thoughts away from Jean, but she continued to press herself into his thinking. Something about her had rammed into his guts like wild fire, and it just kept burning there.

CHAPTER FIVE

As Johnny was sipping on his second drink, he once again found himself wondering about Jean and wanting to know why she had acted so strangely. On the surface she was nothing but a little a porn-chick that stuck herself on any rooster willing to take her on, even in front of a camera. Why had he let her get to him? What did it mean, anyway? Maybe it was merely that seeing her naked, being laid on screen, and being so close in the flesh, so available, made him care. He was totally confused. And completely unable to read her. His body had raced like fire at the thought of doing some of the things with her that the man on the screen had been doing.

Angrily he took a swallow of the drink in his hand and tried to close his mind.

Suddenly it occurred to him that what Jean had told him about his uncle's business activities hadn't really sunk in, hadn't had the effect it should have had.

Maybe the shock of the film, and his emotional involvement in the little scene he was playing out with Jean, had numbed the effects.

Now that he considered it, he had really mixed

reactions.

Johnny wasn't naïve enough to be shocked about what he'd learned tonight; but he was unnerved by it all. Everything was so ironically different from what he'd expected. Instead of walking into a Hollywood film industry, he had sunk into a porno factory cesspool—a step down from where he'd been in the last years. Up or down it was in the same kind of ugly social territory of sex, sin, vice and every other sordid element the world at large enjoyed secretly behind locked doors. Maybe more money to be actually made, but not any less sordid. And certainly, maybe outright illegal.

He knew little about his uncle except for the few things his father had told him over the years. But the information had merely been on the personal side; nothing about Ben Henderson's business life.

Johnny had known about stag movies most of his adult life, but until this night had never seen one. The consideration of what kind of money might be involved in their production had never entered his mind.

After the shock of all this input, his mind surged back, trying to see things on a more realistic, cool level. Business was business. Society was structured in a number of levels, most in shadowy half-worlds, socially accepted as part of a hidden world people didn't talk about. The law looked the other way, pay-offs were offered, and more importantly, political favors given to powerful men who craved a far richer sensual experience than was commonly accepted as proper. Sex and drugs were only a part of the picture. Most of these men wanted women outside of marriage, wanted to play with no strings attached. And the women, like those who had kept him alive and well over the years, enjoyed their secret boy-toys on the side. He knew this world and could play it quite easily.

So, why all the shock?

He shrugged, trying to put it all together, accept things as they were.

He looked around at the room, then at the bookcases lined with books. Standing, he started scanning the titles. Then he came to several titles that were unsubtly erotic.

Love and Sin. The Sadistic Miss Johnston. Butcher Me a Man.

My Kitten Is Hot Over You!

He pulled out a book entitled, *The Bitch of Lord Baymore.*

Opening the book, he was immediately faced with a picture of a man and woman in a very erotic position. He flipped open the first page of the book.

The study door opened. He looked up, slamming the book shut.

Laura Henderson was standing there. On her face was a thick light of amusement.

"Well, you sure screwed that party up!" she announced.

"So…screw you."

"Darling, that was what it was all about. Not getting screwed!" Her voice was thick and the words slurred slightly. The bright gleam in her eyes had been caused by too many drinks, downed much too fast. "Jean's a nice girl! You're an ass!"

"What's that make you?" he snapped, angrily.

"At least I'm being honest. You're just being a shit!"

"You could have warned me."

"Why? It was more fun this way. She's something wild! And you blew it! About time you faced up to how things are!"

"And just how is that?"

She crossed the room and stopped before him. Her right hand reached up and turned the book around so that she could read the title.

She laughed nastily. "A good dirty book. And I thought you were shocked over the film!"

"I was pissed! And you can guess why!" he retorted.

"Well, read on. If that turns you on! You might learn something from it, dear." She was drunk. "I don't think you really know how to treat a lady!"

"Don't push it! I'm not in the mood!"

She laughed. "And that book is going to make you nicer? I'd have thought you could be a bit smarter than you were tonight! I really hoped you'd like Jean. I figured it might help us…get a little distance. Don't say I didn't try."

There was something about the way she was staring at him, the way her body moved, the expression in her eyes that screamed all too loudly what might happen next.

"You've had too much to drink."

"Yes. Of course. Too much drinking. But the wrong kind of cocktail!" She laughed as if having said something very dirty. "Those fuck films made me hungry for a real man. It's too bad you don't know when a woman wants it bad!"

"What's with you? I thought we'd decided to cut this kind of thing out!"

"Screw you. I tried to fix you up. I tried to divert

you with Jean. And look what happened?"

He turned away. "Come on, Laura, he nice.

"Don't you want me?" Laura invited, huskily. "Or are you simply afraid? Or did some bitch cut it off?"

"Cool it, Laura! Before it goes too far!" Johnny snapped.

Laughter mocked him, coarse and wanton. "I don't think it matters any more."

"Where are your other guests?" he asked, controlling his own thick tongue, hoping to change the subject.

"Gone. You broke up a hot party, I'm afraid," she announced bitterly, though there was a sharp change in her aggressive attitude as if she'd realized it wouldn't get her anywhere. "Jean wanted to leave. And Larry, having brought her, did as instructed."

He merely shrugged that off.

"The party was a dud anyway. But it does leave us alone, doesn't it?"

He jerked his head toward her and the expression on his face cut her speech off.

Laura laughed, winking mockingly.

"Oh shut up!" Johnny snapped.

"Come over here and make me!" Laura snapped, hands on hips, eyes glaring, passionate. "The only way you'll shut me up is to give me a sample of what you've been handing out to all those ladies who kept you!"

"I thought you'd agreed to cool it! You're drunk. Cut it out!" He didn't dare focus on her body. He simply kept his eyes away from her as much as possible.

"Drunk yes, and more! I'm a passionate woman,

Jack. And I think game time is over! There's nothing wrong with being passionate." She stepped closer. Her hand caressed his arm. "You have hard muscles."

Laura's lips moved close to his. "I'm sorry about insulting you."

He could feel her hot breath burning his cheek.

She grinned slightly. "I'm a little surprised at your prudishness about all this. I thought you were a little more sophisticated!"

Johnny stepped back, away from her. "That wasn't sophistication in there!"

Laura laughed, twisted around on one heel, and then faced him again. "Hardly, was it?"

She laughed again, glided over to the bar and fixed herself a drink.

"Hardly, was it?" she repeated, staring at him. "But it sure was sexy. What a blow-job she gave out to that guy!"

Johnny threw the book onto the chair, hoping somehow to toss aside the fury building up inside him. "For Christ's sake!"

"I'm delighted with you, Jack," she cried, the forced laughter still in her voice. "You're really quite cute, you know. Trying to play the so-so-tough, the man of the world, and you're nothing but a frightened little boy. Why, I bet that reputation you have with women is all bull!"

Johnny cursed under his breath, his eyes automatically studying Laura's figure.

She wore a flaring skirt; her low-cut blouse showed more of her breasts than it should have. Earlier she had worn a blue jacket that matched the skirt.

74

"I bet you wouldn't know what to do if I just decided to strip naked and throw myself into your arms!" she taunted

"Don't try it! Auntie Laura!" Johnny warned, feeling the blood beginning to race through him. With any other woman he would have willingly given her what she wanted.

'We're back to the Aunt Laura stage, are we?" she mocked. "Something should be done about that!"

She dropped her hands and before he realized what was happening, her skirt fell to the floor about her feet.

"Now look at what you've made me do!" she laughed as if in shocked surprise. "I bet I don't look like an aunt to you now, do I?"

Johnny turned and started for the door.

"Johnny boy, look at me..." she sang lightly.

He turned to see her pulling off her blouse.

With an angry curse he rushed out of the room and up the steps. A moment later he was leaning against the door of his room.

He wiped sweat from his forehead.

"God, what'd I get myself into now?" he breathed.

After a moment he crossed the room, opened the balcony door and moved outside.

The cool air of the summer night soothed his body, caressed the dampness from his face. He stood there, holding onto the hand rail, looking out across Los Angeles stretching below him like a sea of jewels spread on black velvet.

He didn't know how long he stood there before the sound of his bedroom door opening turned his attention to the room.

"Johnny-boy, where are you?" Laura's voice called. She was drunk, her words thick but laughing.

Laura was standing in the middle of the room staring at him, a crooked grin on her pouting lips. She was stark naked.

The blood throbbed through his body and in his temples.

"You goddamned whore!" he cursed between tightly clenched teeth as he stepped into the bedroom, softly closing the balcony door behind him.

"Damned right, love!" She opened her arms to him and pressed her lush body forward. Their lips met, open, moist, the points of their tongues embracing like warm fire. She strained to him, and when their long kiss broke, she moaned softly in his ear. "God, how I want you—every moment since you walked into this house!"

Laura led him to the large bed and lay down, waiting, watching as he slowly undressed.

"Big boy, come to auntie," she invited in a low moan, stretching out her arms.

He slid down to her, and after that didn't think about anything except the soft warm body that seemed to wrap around his. Hands caressed, thighs and legs locked in place in such a natural way that it was unnerving. They simply seemed to fit in a rage of wild passion.

Their lips greedily feasted on one another's. She was wantonly totally out of control. Her body was a shivery sea of heat as it moved against his. Soft moans murmured from deep within the woman as she tensed, lifted, and then seemed to fold around him like a lovely warm vice.

Now there was no waiting, for the days leading up to this moment had built the tension to the bursting point. It was like attempting to escape some kind of velvet trap, almost making it, then being yanked swiftly back.

All at once Laura screamed. After that her lips merely moaned.

He knew this was only a beginning.

Laura was a feasting hunger and a driving force that would devour any man within reach. She had won her battle for him. And he had, in the end, willingly submitted to the full carnal desire she inspired.

Laura sobbed at times, and gasped, moaned, muttered wordless sounds, as her touches, kisses, body commanded his to match her own needs. The fury passions subsided to more longer, lingering, loving connections. She became a continual wave of desire, a continual series of soft, and velvety warm touches, electric caresses that softly enveloped him within her total embrace. He never knew when it all ended, faded, all he knew was the gentle flow of pleasure that finally closed about his consciousness

* * * * * * *

Johnny slowly turned on his side and felt the soft form of a woman lying next to him in the large bed. For a moment he couldn't remember who she was. The dream that had awakened him had left his mind miles away, dazed and fogged. The hangover throbbed his head like hammers.

He sat up, startled, remembering.

Looking down at Laura, he felt a pang of desire begin to stir through him. She was a wonderful, graceful lover; a soft, throbbing female animal.

It had been an amazing experience; something he had not expected.

The raven black hair rested on the white pillow around her sleeping face. She looked much younger, almost childlike in sleep. Her lips were relaxed, full and velvet looking. Lipstick had smeared off her mouth, and rich natural wine color she looked even more bewitching.

His mind relived the long hours they had made love, the variety of her imagination when it came to finding new ways toward the passionate completion of their hungers. She was an uninhibited woman. And everything they had shared in that bed was a series of wildly erotic sensations—not so much tender as electrically alive. Yet in the end she'd been amazing, a continual wave of mere pleasure ebbing throughout his whole body. He just remembered that sensation drifting over him until consciousness had faded.

Amazing.

She stirred and opened her eyes. Her lips trembled under his and as he started to lift his head, her hands pressed his head down again. Her mouth was a wide cavern, waiting for the point of his tongue, drawing it deep beyond her teeth. He felt her tongue press his against the roof of her mouth, as if it were some delicacy of which she could never tire. Finally they broke apart and she sat up.

"You taste good," she murmured, nestling against chest. "Real good."

Johnny caressed her jet black hair, near the base of her skull. They lay there for some time, silently aware of each other. It was a silence filled with full communication that only two lovers who have found complete sensual joy with one another can enjoy. Finally she turned, resting her head on his lap, looking up at him.

"I was wrong about you," she observed, wrinkling her delicate nose.

"How's that?" Johnny knew his voice was faraway, distant.

"You know your way around women."

"You never believed differently." His fingers slid through her hair.

"Maybe not. Maybe not." She was thoughtful. "But after the scene last night—I mean tonight, earlier—I had begun to doubt that—"

"Let's not talk about it!" he snapped, moving his hand down to the curve of her right breast. Laura tensed.

"What you want to talk about, honey Jack?" she murmured, her eyes half closed.

"Maybe about you. Maybe about Uncle Ben. Maybe about nothing." He looked into her eyes, which had suddenly jerked open when he'd mentioned her husband.

"What do you want to know about me and Ben? That we are a failure as husband and wife? That he can't satisfy me sexually? That he's cold—or steps out on me?" she inquired in a completely bland voice.

"Well?"

"It's not quite true."

"I didn't think so." His hand cupped her breast and gently rolled the soft, supple flesh.

"What do you think, then?" She pushed his hand from her breast and sat up, staring seriously at him.

79

"I don't know." Johnny reached for a pack of cigarettes on the bedstand. He lighted two and placed one between Laura's lips. "What is the story?"

"Don't you think that's pretty personal?" she snapped, whipping the cigarette from her lips. Her mouth was suddenly hard, her eyes narrow.

"Hardly, after last night, after what we've done." He dragged deep on the cigarette and looked at the far wall. The conversation was annoying both of them, but he realized there was no way around it now. "I'm sorry I brought it up."

She sighed. "What do you want to know, Jack?"

"Just enough to relieve my mind—to know what this means, and where I stand. Quite simple." He looked evenly at her.

Silence fell on the room, becoming as dark as the night outside. The sound of a car moving along the street broke the silence.

In the semi-gloom, Johnny watched the rising and falling of Laura's breasts as she struggled in some inner battle with herself. Finally her breasts heaved high and then fell, as she took a deep breath and sighed it out.

"Okay, I'll start from the beginning." She stabbed out the cigarette in an ash tray.

"I met your uncle about seven years ago. I was a struggling actress, making B-movies and getting nowhere. I happened to be at a party; Ben was there and we got to talking. He made a pass, which I ignored, and then he stopped attempting to be sexy. That intrigued me. After a few drinks and a few hours of conversation, he invited me out for a drive. The party was dull and boring; everybody was already thinning out. We left, drove down to the beach and parked. At first I thought Ben was going to play the teenage game of necking his way into a sexual relationship in the car. He was strictly hands off. It annoyed me. He said little about his work, and even when I asked him about it, he refused to tell me much. Merely that he put together films for private distribution. By two in the morning he drove me to my apartment and made arrangements for a date.

"On the third date we went to bed together. He's not a very good lover. A little too quick. I don't know how things got so involved. But suddenly I was in love with him, and a few months later we got married." She hesitated and then added: "I still love him."

"But you go out for other men—because he can't give you everything you want."

Her silence answered him for a long time. Then she said, "I wouldn't let him know about what happened tonight. I mean—between us."

"Relatives are out?" Johnny asked, not surprised.

"*Everybody* is out. If he knew I was cheating on him, he'd hit the roof. He doesn't know." She sounded worried. "Believe me—he doesn't know!"

"Come on, Laura—you couldn't keep such things from him. Hell, with a man like Larry Jenkins and all those other people around—you don't think he's a fool—or that they would keep quiet about what was going on behind his back."

Her hand slapped across his face and she jerked up in bed. Her face was contorted with fury.

Johnny leaped from the bed, yanked her down

onto it and pinned her arms to her sides. "Don't ever hit me again, Laura. Don't you ever do that again!"

Terror worked into her eyes and her lips trembled. It was several minutes before either of them moved or said anything. "I...I keep quiet, Jack, about things that happen. Nothing would have... happened at the party. We were just taking a look at Jean's new movie—that's all. Everybody knew about you and Jean. I mean. That was a set-up for you to get...well, never mind. That blew up. But they don't know about me."

"But I do."

"That was a mistake!" Her voice was harsh and strong again. "Let me up, Jack!"

Slowly he lifted from her and slid over to his side of the bed.

They were silent for a long time.

"I'm sorry, Laura. Really."

"I'm sorry, too. I couldn't help myself. The drinks made me a bitchy." Suddenly she collapsed in his arms, hugging to him, soft sobs breaking from her lips. "I'm suddenly afraid—terribly afraid, Jack. Please help me. Please help me!"

Johnny felt nothing emotionally toward Laura as he cradled her against him, gently caressing her back, murmuring softly that everything would be all right. All he could think of was the fire of her body and the way it hungrily devoured him in ecstasy. Yet it was this very element that caused him to comfort her. The bond of their lovemaking had fused a link between them; a link that would never be broken, regardless of what their bodies did or didn't do to each other in the future.

CHAPTER SIX

The night was darkening, the stars blinking out one by one, before Laura finally gained control of her emotions. The mood had changed very slowly from one of intense anguish on Laura's part to intimate awareness of their naked closeness.

Her body was warm against his and it slowly began inching upward. Finally her head was just under his and she jerked her face up so that soft lips pressed against his. The kiss was tenderness at first, but quickly developed into a wanton tension that strained them tightly together.

Laura's hands clawed her body against his. He could feel the damp warmth of her breasts clinging to the flesh of his chest.

Finally the kiss broke, and she slowly pulled him down over her. "Love me, Jack! Love me real good," she murmured.

Johnny felt suddenly sorry for her. He had seldom felt more than physical need for a woman—outside of his momentary pity for Jean Harold.

Gently leaning over Laura, he caressed the tips of her breasts. As he moved tenderly, sensually circling the rosy softness around her nipple, she moaned happily, caressing his arms, writhing.

"Oh, Jack, you're good—good," she told him in a low, throaty voice. "Good—so good!"

Then somehow he was on his back and Laura ran her tongue down over his stomach.

"Oh, I'll love it good!" she moaned.

When she abruptly swung her thigh over him, Johnny frantically began feasting on this woman's flesh like a starving man devouring a delicious banquet.

The sensations were fantastically erotic and loving.

Her hips ground in wide circles and she moaned, tensed as if in orgasm, then continued her rapid movements, making a sort, purring sound of deeply contented pleasure.

How long it lasted, Johnny didn't know. She wasn't merely taking, this time. She was loving him with her whole body.

Finally both of them began sobbing in their mutual need for release. They thrust harshly against one another several dozen times. Then all at once Laura seemed to convulsively squeeze down hard upon him like a vice of velvet steel.

"Oh, you were so good!" she moaned in a weak whisper.

Time drifted. Johnny's thoughts became blurred, sensation numbed.

He became aware of gentle movement and soft female flesh against his own. A mental picture of Jean Harold formed momentarily before his half-conscious mind.

What happened after that was distant, without any real form. He realized that a woman was making love to him, and responded automatically in a kind of half-sleep. It was like having a sexual dream. The woman's body was nothing more than a sex form. The sensations that needled their way through his nerves seemed remote, though actively alive. It was like dreaming. In fact, he really wasn't sure it wasn't a dream.

Somehow it didn't matter.

His mind continued to picture Jean Harold. The whole thing became puzzling and confused because he knew who touched and kissed and finally wrapped herself around him in a wild moment of lustful passion.

The whole thing held no immediate meaning to him.

Even the climax was as if it were waving through another person, as if his mind were detached from his body.

"Jack—Jack—oh, God—Jack!" he heard her cry out in intense pain and pleasure. Her hands were clawing into his back, the nails digging cruelly, painfully. It was this latter sensation that brought his mind back to what was happening, and the pleasure slammed up like an all-embracing blanket of ecstasy, numbing him.

Moments later he slipped away from Laura and slumped onto his stomach exhausted

It seemed only seconds before a caressing hand moved along his back and a voice said softly like a gentle murmur of silver wind, "Jack, oh, I love your body. It gives me so much pleasure, such wonderful pleasure. I've never known a man like you—never in my life." Arms slid under his chest and he felt warm velvety flesh hugging his back. "I love every muscle in it!"

She laid there, her chest pressed into his back, her cheek against his shoulder, clinging to him as if it were for the last time.

"I'm glad you came into my life. So wonderful—so wonderful!" she murmured into his ear. "We're good together, aren't we? You said we were alike. Oh, how it is the truth."

"Cut it out!" Johnny snapped, forcefully turning and facing her. "Cut it out!"

She frowned, her face anguished. The fear of losing him was written on every tightly pinched feature of her delicate face.

He sat up and gently moved her back to her side of the bed. "I don't like to be possessed!"

"Oh, that's it?" Her voice was dull, lifeless. "I'm sorry, Jack. I'll never be possessive with you. Never. I promise. I promise!" Her eyes searched his. "Please, Jack—understand. I never knew anything like you before—never! It overwhelms me."

"We better forget it. You're married—to my uncle. Like you said before, if he ever found out...it's too messy!"

Johnny stood and went to the huge glass doorway that opened out to the balcony. The sun was beginning to peek over the eastern horizon, lighting the smog of Los Angeles, revealing the dirty haze that hung over the city like a plague of filth.

"What are you talking about?" Laura's voice was desperate.

He turned, looked at her. Laura was clutching the bed sheets, staring at him through wide, frowning eyes. The expression on her face was wild desperation; a desperation of a woman possessed with emotional needs and physical hungers she can't control.

"We cut it out—before things are too thick to stop!" he told her in a firm, impersonal voice. "Quit while we're ahead."

Her throat contracted and she swallowed hard on some tightness there. Her green eyes lowered to the bed.

He watched the quick rising and falling of her breasts until they calmed in their heavy rhythm. Then he slowly stepped over to her and gently placed an arm around her shoulder.

"You know I'm right, Laura. You said earlier that it was a mistake—and it was! More than you realized. All we can do is laugh it off as over-strain after a pretty hot movie—and too many drinks. Forget it, and try to act like it was some wild, insane dream."

"But it wasn't."

"You were lovely. It was great. That's it. We have to get past this. That's the reality."

She twisted and stared up at him. Her mouth hung open for a moment and then closed. Her eyes slowly went dead.

"You're right, I guess," she said in a dull voice. Slowly she slipped from the bed, and walked gracefully across the room, to the door. She turned and looked at him for a moment. "I don't know if I can ever forget—or want to not have that beautiful body of yours—"

"Next time I won't give in, Laura. Try to do the same thing."

She laughed hollowly, almost mockingly. "Don't be a damned fool, Jack. You know we won't act like it never happened, that it won't happen again."

She was in control of herself, the woman who had marched into his room the night before, naked and challenging, demanding. "We've just begun—and that I promise you. You're too good to keep away from! I want you, and I'll have you—anytime I snap my fingers!"

Johnny felt ice crawl into his stomach as she left the room. Her sudden outburst had almost been bordering on madness. It was almost paranoid. He stared at the closed door and found it hard to control the sudden shaking of his nerves.

For some time he stood beside the bed, staring at the door. Then finally he found his clothing on the floor where he'd thrown it the night before. Dressing quickly, Johnny went to the balcony and found the small staircase that led to the ground. A moment later he slipped behind the wheel of his Ford and started down the curving road.

His mind was numbed, almost terrified at what had happened with Laura Henderson, and a little awed that he felt such an emotional reaction.

He drove down Santa Monica, then north along Highway 101, and finally found a parking place, got out of the car, and walked along the sand for some distance before he sat down a few yards away from the water, gazing out across the blue-gray of the Pacific Ocean.

He had come out west to find a new life for himself, to change his luck, to run away from a past that had been nothing but failure and bumming it with women. And already he'd managed to get himself involved with a sex-hungry broad who just happened to be his uncle's wife. That was all he needed.

The bitterness choked in him and sudden tears started to water his eyes, slowly running down his cheeks.

"Goddam the ever-loving world. And crap on women!" He stood and kicked off his shoes, pulled off his socks, rolled up his pants. A moment later he was treading water.

His mind turned to Jean Harold and what had gone on between them, the night before.

They had played around with a game of trying to find understanding. A game that was usually reserved for people interested in each other; not for two strangers.

Yet, as he thought about her, he realized that there was a strange, subconscious awareness between them; what it was, he didn't quite know.

But one thing he suddenly knew. He wanted to see Jean Harold again. If for no other reason than to take the bitter taste of Laura off his mind and body and out of his mouth.

"Boy, Johnny, you really screwed things—like always! Screwed Laura Henderson—and screwed yourself! A great start on a new future! A real great start!" He cursed to himself. Stopping ankle deep in the water, Johnny pulled out a pack of cigarettes from his shirt pocket and lighted one. He stood there until it was finished, then throwing the lighted butt into the ocean he turned.

Returning to his car, he headed back to Beverly Hills. An hour later he entered the long hallway of his uncle's house.

A tall, thick-boned man was standing in the middle of the room, talking to Laura. He had steel gray hair. A thin mustache lined his long upper lip. His eyes, when they turned to look at Johnny, were light gray, steel hard, but had an underlining sensitivity about them as they appraised Johnny.

He grinned, his lips spreading wide over thick, even teeth.

"So you're Bess's son. You look just like your father when he was a young man. Just like your father."

Johnny stepped forward and forced a smile. "So you're Uncle Henderson!"

"Ben—Ben. It's good to know you, son—good to know you!" Ben Henderson placed a heavy arm around Johnny and hugged him close. "Good to know you."

For an awkward moment the room was silent. Then Ben Henderson looked at his wife. "Well, dear, how about leaving us alone, to talk over a few things. We don't even know each other, and there's a lot to learn..." He squeezed Johnny tighter and then stepped away.

As Laura stood, Ben Henderson patted her fanny and laughed. "She's a real looker, isn't she, Johnny?"

Johnny nodded and stood there in the middle of the room, fighting an inner struggle. This large, robust stranger was a man he knew little about; the man who might be able to help him get a new start in life. His mother's half of the family.

* * * * * * *

Ben Henderson took a thick cigar from his inside coat pocket, slowly lighted it and settled heavily down on the sofa, looking at Johnny.

"You're a lot like your mother—a lot like your father. Seems strange, meeting after all this time, doesn't it, Johnny?"

Ben Henderson stood, spread his arms in the air and shrugged.

"How about us having a couple of drinks and getting to really know each other. We have a lot to talk about and plan."

Johnny followed Ben into the study. The doors were closed and bolted.

"Privacy—from the world. This is my little hideaway. When I come in here—well, it's my world. Nobody touches it, or me." He mixed drinks, handed Johnny one and then downed his in three swallows. He refilled his empty glass. "Well, my boy, we gotta think of what you want to do. All I know is that you need a place—a direction, from what your letters say. How about you talking now?"

Johnny studied his uncle for a moment and then walked to the chair in the corner, sitting down. He didn't know the man. Jean had said he was a bastard who introduced her to porno film-making and was, himself, a producer of such packages. That really shouldn't bother him. But it did. And yet the man seemed so damned friendly. Very warm. From what Laura had claimed, he was loveable.

Johnny didn't know what to believe, but decided to give the man at least a fair chance.

"I don't know what I want—now." He hesitated and then decided to clear the air. "I saw one of your movies light night."

Ben frowned and then sighed. "What do you want me to say? I had wished to break that in on you a little more slowly. If at all. How'd it happen?"

"Your wife had a little party, and, well, they showed a movie with Jean Harold in it. Jean was here—more or less coupled for me."

"How'd you like the girl?" His uncle beamed. The expression on his face was quite openly lecherous.

"Nothing happened, if that's what you mean." Johnny felt irritation creep through him.

"I'm sorry. Surprised."

"I couldn't swallow that film and the whole set-up."

"I'm surprised."

"And disappointed?"

"Not at all. Business…all that. But I'd have expected you to be rather…casual about such matters. Considering your life style."

"That's another thing completely. I didn't know anything about…the business. Stag films and all that."

"Yes…I suppose that was a bit of a surprise." The man studied him for a moment, then said: "Yes, it's a dirty business, I'll admit that. But there's money in it. A lot of money in it. But that's not the only business I'm operating. There's the club and, well, I thought maybe you could start there. Work as a sorta charm-boy…just sorta an assistant manager. Maybe at $250.00 a week?" The grin was wide, overwhelming; filled with a powerful charm that was disarming. "Nothing illegal. Nothing you can't handle. And I really want to give you a start. We're related. Blood. And you are important to me. I want to set you up right. Get you into something different from what you've been doing. Why not? I'm anxious to get you settled and in the pink of things."

Johnny stared at his uncle and then sighed. There wasn't any other place for him to go. Returning to the life he'd led in the last few years would be more of a hell than taking this opportunity from his uncle. The fact that Henderson made money by producing stag movies wasn't his business.

Either he took the offer, or bummed again with the life he was running away from. Once he had a place of his own, Laura wouldn't be a serious issue.

"I don't get you, Ben. Not at all."

"Those movies? Right?"

"I suppose so."

"Well, it is a mere investment. Money. Merely money. And if I don't do it somebody else does. I run a clean business there. The girls are well kept. And they get out of it when they want. I…well, never mind. Somebody is going to do it—my not doing it won't stop it. I might as well join in."

Johnny looked away from his uncle. For a moment he had the impulse to tell the man to go to hell. Then the more practical side of his mind took over.

"Okay—but I get a pad of my own. Any objection?" Johnny stood.

"No objection. Though I'd rather you stay here for a little while. At least until you get settled in the job." Ben stepped forward and patted Johnny on the shoulder. "You know, I think I like you. You'll be okay. Real okay?" A frown formed on his face. "You don't let that film thing bother you. It has nothing to do with what you'll be involved with. I have a lot of business interests. Right on the up and above board level. Okay?"

Johnny forced a grin, shrugged. "What you do,

that's not my concern. Thanks."

"Now...how about another drink, a little friendly chatting and, tell me, how're you fixed for women?" A gleam lighted in Ben's eyes. "I can set you up for some real cuties. Any time. Any time at all."

"Might tell me how I can get hold of Jean—"

"Any time. Arrange everything. Tomorrow I'll take you to the club. She works there, anyway. A cocktail waitress."

"I thought she was a—"

"An actress? A struggling one. That's why she did the film. Wanted a little money, a start. I told her to do the film and I'd do a real picture for her." Ben laughed.

"And—you'll do the real thing—for her?" Johnny felt an edge of anger stem its way up through him.

"Someday, someday soon, Maybe. It all depends."

Johnny tensed. His face was flushing with anger. For a moment he stood there, not sure why he was so angry. "You mean you conned her—?"

"No! No! Nothing like that, sonny." Ben's arm slapped around Johnny. "She gets into something. Just don't you worry about my business, and I won't get into yours. Okay?"

When Johnny finally got up to his room he was slightly drunk. He lay on the bed, confused by the storming thoughts racing through his mind.

His uncle was a somewhat strange and degenerate man. That much Johnny had quickly made up his mind about. But there was more to it than simply that side. Laura, for all her faults, claimed to love him with all his faults.

And, Johnny realized, what right did he have to judge the man. His own life had been rather on the deeply shady side. So, if the man was into some questionable business, that was his affair. And if Jean was being played; that was her problem. The woman was over twenty-one and old enough to know what she wanted.

Then he remembered how she'd cried, how he'd wanted to protect her, hold her, be so very tenderly caring. It all didn't make sense. He was totally off balance about everything.

A thought of running out of the deal raced through his mind; he quickly pushed aside the impulse.

"Snap out of it!" he told himself. "The real world was a nasty setup for anybody—and you survived any way you could. Ben Henderson was offering a free ride to easy success. And Johnny realized the life he'd been leading was a ride to nowhere fast. Here he had a chance to start fresh and get some solid grounding.

He could get a new start. A night club job might be just the type of deal he needed. One thing for sure, he wouldn't get fired. He had an inside track to get into a business of his own. Running a night club could satisfy several of his personal hungers—emotionally, physically and mentally. The next afternoon after lunch, Ben Henderson drove Johnny through Beverly Hills and then into Los Angeles. It was well past three by the time they arrived at a small strip joint.

Johnny was surprised to discover the type of night club his uncle owned, but wasn't bothered by it. In fact the idea was intriguing.

The place, this time of day, was completely deserted. But the posters, advertising the strippers, promised a grand show in the true sensual tradition.

"What about these girls?" Johnny asked over the Scotch and soda his uncle had mixed for him. They were sitting at the bar, overlooking the stage and the customer's tables. "Their social life?"

Ben grinned and shrugged. "Same as other girls."

Johnny frowned, puzzled. "I thought they—well, either picked up with the studs, easy like, or played the hustler game."

"Nothing like that, Johnny. They have to take care of their bodies. Look at them as dancers. And most of them were, in the beginning. They come to the big city, knock around town a few months, maybe years, with stars in their eyes, with hunger for lights. And they end up dancing for strip places. Anything to get a start. Only thing is, they stay, most of them. The business pays enough to keep them going. A good stripper can make a mint, but there aren't too many. Some girls act so bored that they wouldn't excite a sex maniac!"

Johnny sipped his drink and looked the place over. There was a purple curtain that covered the small stage. A little section to the right of the stage served for a three-piece combo—the only thing in evidence now was the bass, drums and piano.

"So none of them put out?" Johnny asked, turning back to Ben Henderson.

"Now I didn't say that, sonny. I didn't say that at all!"

"Which ones do?"

"Interested?"

"I don't know. That Gloria Sparks on the poster outside—with those knockers, I'd give a week's pay to get at them! Does she spark?"

Ben grinned and nodded. "Play your teeth into that dame and you're in for something wild."

They were silent after that, finishing their drinks. Then Ben took him into an office in the back of the club.

"This is where you'll work, with Joe Carter. He's my manager. He'll teach you the ropes. But watch out for him. He has it big and hard for Gloria—if you're planning on pushing it to her."

"You said something about Jean Harold working here—"

"Want to play poke-chop with her?"

Johnny laughed. For the first time since he'd met his uncle, he almost liked the man. Ben Henderson, regardless of what he did for a living or who he might use, was likeable. A man's man, in a way.

"What do you expect me to do for $250 a week?"

"Learn. Just hang around and watch and learn. Find out how things are run. If you want to make it with some of the girls, do it on your own time."

"How do I get to first base, without playing a few pitches while they're at work?"

"Play the pitches, but don't overplay. I'm not paying you to make it with broads. Just don't try goofing off! Relative or not, I'll expect you to work for your pay. Or I'll kick your ass in! Understand?" The serious quality of the man's voice startled Johnny.

"Sure. You won't regret it."

"I don't expect to. You've bummed your life

away long enough. About time you settled down to something that will give direction. You need a break, so you're getting it. But you work your ass off for it. Nothing in life comes free—the sooner you learn that, the better it will be for you. I came up the hard way, but you're getting in easy." Ben laughed then, but it was a hollow sound, forced, an awkward attempt to break through the seriousness that had choked in around them. "Anyway, sonny, just keep your eyes open, learn, and in a few weeks—or months—we'll be talking some more turkey about the new club!"

They stayed there for the rest of the afternoon, while Ben told Johnny some of the facts about the business and the legal end of the club. By six-thirty they went out to eat at a small restaurant. When they returned to the club, Joe Carter was there.

Carter was a thin, nervous man with a hawk nose; he chewed his cigarette filters and talked in a high, nasal voice.

He shook hands with Johnny and said how glad he was to meet him. But his dark, deep-set eyes were emotionless. Ben Henderson left half an hour later.

Carter took Johnny around the club again showing him details that his uncle had missed. It was well past seven before Johnny was left alone. Carter had told him to help himself to booze, but to keep sober.

By seven-thirty some of the help started wandering in.

He recognized several of the strippers from the posters that advertised them on the outside of the club. When Gloria Sparks arrived, Johnny watched her huge, hefty body wiggle across the room. She was large boned, tall and beefy. Sex wiggled with every move she made.

As Gloria passed him where he was sitting at the bar, he said, "Aren't you Miss Sparks?"

She turned and looked at him coldly. "Yes. And what are you doing here?"

"I'm the new help."

Her eyes moved over his trim body. She was taller than Johnny by a good inch, and much bigger. The idea of being embraced by her lush body was almost frightening, in a wildly exciting way.

"So?"

"So—I just wanted to introduce myself. Jack Belton." He grinned, extending his hand. She sure was one stacked-up mountain of hot-looking flesh.

Her face lighted and those thick, over-size sensual lips spread wide. "Oh, you're Ben's nephew, aren't you?"

She gripped his hand, and the contact was all that her body promised; pure raw animal heat.

"I hear you strip a real wild one," Johnny lied, not actually knowing what kind of stripper she really was and not caring.

She appeared pleased. "Watch, tonight. I'll give a few grinds for you. Special hip-work!"

With that she turned and wiggled her way across the: club, disappearing through a curtained doorway.

The three piece combo set themselves up in their little band nook, fingering their instruments, warming up. A few customers strayed in. The waitresses had already started to check in a few minutes before, but Johnny didn't notice Jean.

He turned to Allen, the bartender, and asked, "When does Jean Harold check in?"

"About nine thirty." The man leered at Johnny. "Know her?"

"A little." Johnny turned his attention to the house He watched the musicians until a man stepped out onto the stage with a mike.

"Hello, ladies and gents, welcome to the Club Tropic." His eyes wandered over the three male customers sitting around the stage tables. "Things are going to be real hot tonight. We got some real live chicks."

"As opposed to dead ones?" a male voice asked.

"Live and Hot! A promise! And for our first number, I'd like you to give a big hand for a lovely little lady, Anne Hot Hips."

The band riffed into a slow *"I Can't Get Started with You,"* and the stage curtains opened. A tiny, dark-haired girl stepped onto stage in a red evening gown. She gracefully moved in rhythm to the slow beat of the number, smiling at the three lone customers in that purely professional way that strippers have of not appearing in the least bit sexy. Her actions were automatic, without emotion. The expression in her eyes was boredom.

Anne whipped through a series of grinding, bumping attempts to appear as though she were having sexual intercourse; but, as before, didn't come across with any real excitement. When she was finished, Johnny sighed out his relief, and felt the audience was just as glad.

The MC reappeared on stage.

"Isn't she a wonder? Just started last week. Her first engagement in Los Angeles. Give the little darling another hand."

A scatter of polite clapping followed.

"Now we got a real number that will start things off with hot fire. Little Red Riding Hood! Betty Bumps."

A blonde appeared on stage. Her first chorus was routine, the second a little more interesting. She didn't have much breast development for a stripper, but what she had, she used to good advantage. When she wound up her act with a wild contortion of wiggles, bumps and grinds, the audience, which had grown to about fifteen people, mostly men, went wild.

"How do you like the show?" a familiar feminine voice inquired at Johnny's side.

Johnny turned to find himself facing Jean Harold.

"Well, I was looking forward to seeing you again."

To Johnny's surprise, he felt a tingle of excitement at seeing Jean. She was dressed in a white blouse, open at the top, and a flaring gray skirt. She looked like any nice young kid.

"Have you forgotten the other night?" she asked, acidly.

Johnny managed to shrug off her remark. "Let's forget the other night. Start all over again."

Her eyes questioned him in a puzzled way.

"I'm Jack Belmont And what's your name?" She grinned "Jean. Glad to meet you Jack"

"How about us cutting out after work?"

She looked shocked. "You mean to pick me up? Why, Jack, what kind of girl do you think I am?"

"What kind of guy do you think I am? I promise

to do nothing you wouldn't want me to! More, I promise you'll remain in the same virginal condition you are in right now."

She did a double take on that, uncertain as to how he meant that.

"Well, you'll remain same virgin you are right now!"

She then laughed at that. "You're kinda funny tonight!"

"Well? You consider me safe enough to spend a little time with? I only have typical male designs on…"

"Stop right there, before you terrify me!" she laugh.

"Well? I promise to a boring, perfect gentleman!"

"You…boring? I doubt it!"

"Well, a perfect gentleman, anyway."

"Of sorts, right?"

"Right. Of sorts. But seriously. How about it?"

She laughed softly again, turned, picked up a tray with drinks on it that Allen had placed on the bar.

"See you later." She whipped away, adding: "It's a date."

Johnny felt a swell of hot excitement. Suddenly he realized how much he really wanted to get to know Jean—he actually liked her!

CHAPTER SEVEN

Johnny hardly noticed the strippers for the next hour.

It wasn't until the club had been fairly well filled, and Gloria Sparks was announced, that he paid any attention.

Gloria was squeezed into the tightest fitting glittering silver gown she could have possibly gotten into. Her breasts were flowing over the restraining neckline.

She stood in the middle of the stage, looking over the audience.

"I see we have some real lovers of the art," she murmured in a low, husky voice. "You want to see mama strip?"

There were shouts from the audience.

"Can't hear you, boys."

"Take it off!" somebody shouted.

"Why, baby, what kind of girl do you think I am?" she said in an innocent, mocking voice. She pouted, thrust her huge chest out, leaned over and wiggled. "That what you wanna see mama do?"

She grinned, moistened her lips with the point of a pink tongue, and then straightened again.

She nodded to the band, which broke into a slow

arrangement of *Old Black Magic*. Then she started walking around the stage. Her movement was graceful, animal. She had an air about her that was startling in its sensuality. Every action had controlled sex in it. Slowly, as if struggling to restrain herself, she began slipping out of the long gloves that reached up over her elbows. Every move of her fingers became sensual caresses, and little shivers seemed to tremble along her flesh. It was quite convincing. Then as the number was coming to a close, she slipped out of her dress, in one bold, swift move.

The audience whistled, yelled, laughed. She stood before them and jerked her hips into a bump and grind that the drummer accented with cymbals. She was dressed in tight bra and panties. Her breasts were about as large as they could get without overloading her. Johnny had never seen anything quite so amazing as Gloria Sparks.

"Now what you want, guys? Wanna to see my little knockers?"

A male voice shouted: "They ain't little, baby!"

"How'd you know? Did you peek?" she swiftly countered with a shocked smile. "Shame on you!"

The audience laughed at that, and there were a few boos added to the mix.

She frowned. "Is that for my baby knockers?"

She wigged, causing her breasts to vibrate wildly.

"Want to see if they're real?" she teased, bending over so that the audience had a full view of her breasts. She wiggled, and the soft flesh of her breasts wiggled like supple jelly.

The band played *Black Magic* again, but this

time with a wild Latin beat.

Gloria started dancing, moving her hips, her breasts, with every beat of the music. The audience went wild.

Johnny felt the reaction in his body at the sight of Gloria. Her long blonde hair flowed over her shoulders, waving with every action she made. Just looking made him want her any time any day.

Slowly she jerked out of her bra and those huge melons surged forward, naked except for the stars covering their large nipples. She slipped out of her outer panties and then started to really go to work. Her lips kept throwing kisses at the audience, and she played her hips into the faces of several male customers. And one female.

At that point she cried: "Oh, sorry. You're not my type!"

That got a laugh.

"You ain't hers!" the man next to the woman countered throatily, his eyes fasted on her boobs.

"But I bet I'm yours!" She wiggled in the man's face and the audience roared with laughter.

She went through the routine of every stripper since the beginning of time. From the subtle little jerking action of her hips, to the swinging circling of her huge breasts. When she was finished, there was a glistening to her flesh.

Her act was the end of the show, and a short intermission followed.

A few minutes after she had left the stage, Gloria turned up on the stool next to Johnny's, fully dressed.

"How'd you like me?" she breathed into his ear, pressing the point of one of her breasts into his arm.

"You were great!" Johnny found it impossible to keep his eyes off her neckline.

She laughed throatily and then moved her breast away from his arm. "I thought maybe you could come backstage to my room for a drink."

"I'm supposed to stay out here and watch the customers," Johnny managed to say in a controlled voice.

She snickered. "You won't be gone that long."

She squeezed his arm.

Johnny felt a murmur of warning rush through him. What was she after? She'd been ice cold before learning who he was, then she'd thawed and now she was hot, willing fire.

Shrugging, Johnny stepped from the stool and followed Gloria behind stage and into a small dressing room. She closed and bolted the door behind her.

Turning, Gloria studied Johnny. "I hear that your uncle does movies."

Johnny nodded, feeling a tension at the pit of his stomach. She wasn't playing any games about what she wanted. But what puzzled him was why she didn't go directly to Ben Henderson.

"I could use a little extra exposure," Gloria admitted, wiggling across the small room to the dressing table. There was a bottle of whiskey on the table, next to two glasses. "There's a lot of money in that, too. For the smart woman."

"Why talk to me? Why not Uncle Ben?"

She whipped around, her face showing surprise. "I only met him once."

"What?"

"Carter is the man who hires and fires. I merely

do my job. Been here only a few months. I've done everything to get to your uncle. I'll do anything for a real private introduction. Carter has promised, but never comes through." She stepped close to Johnny.

"You know what kind of movies Ben is doing?"

"Stag, of course." A strange light broke into her blue eyes. "Kind of kinky! And could be a career plus for a woman like me."

Johnny felt a thin sense of annoyance. He fought it aside. It wasn't difficult since he couldn't keep his eyes off her lush, overdeveloped body.

"I can't promise anything, Gloria. But maybe I could put in a good word for you!" He felt like a real bastard. He didn't want anything to do with that end of his uncle's business affairs.

"That's all I ask. And I'm a very generous and thankful lady!"

"How thankful?" he countered, letting his eyes glide over her body as if devouring it.

In response, she simply moved in close, and her arms crushed around his neck, lush lips pressed to his, open and moist. The kiss was blatant come-on. Her tongue whipped deep into his mouth, and then urged his deeply into hers. Finally they broke away. She laughed and looked down, pointedly, at him. "You're a big guy—bigger than I thought you'd be."

She pouted, reached out and caressed him. And then withdrew her hand. "Nice, honey. But I can't do much for that right now. We don't have time to do anything."

"I thought—"

"I said a drink, honey. Nothing more. Later. How about after work?"

107

Johnny shook his head. "Sorry, not tonight. Other arrangements."

She pressed against him. Her breasts cushioned to his chest. "Come on, honey—nothing could be that important!"

Her hips circled against his, seeming to almost screw him through the clothing.

"I know what you want, honey," she told him in a very sultry voice. Yet there was something vaguely stagy about her, as if she were going through some well practiced act. "We really don't have time right now."

There was something about her that was both a turn on and a vulgar turn off.

It was impossible to not react.

"Hell with the right time!" he cursed, jerking her to the couch. "To hell with that! We have all the time necessary! I'm management!"

Here eyes arched in surprise. "Come to think of it…so you are."

A hard, hot lump choked his throat.

"Is this what you want?" She reached around to the back of her dress, and suddenly she was standing there half naked. The blood raced like hammers at his temples.

She lay on the couch, her legs spread wide. "Best hurry, honey! Before you lose it all!"

The woman's voice almost mocked him in its challenging laugh.

Johnny didn't even bother removing all of his clothing. When he came down on her, she gripped his rear, pushed him hard against her warm flesh.

"That feels good. Mommy would just love to kiss…you right there! But no time!"

At that point Gloria lifted, taking him deep in her with one skillful move, then started making quick jerking, grinding circles with her hips.

"How you dig that, honey?" she inquired in a tense, though almost casual, voice.

Then suddenly she simply gasped and moaned, almost mechanically. It was difficult to tell what was act and what was real. Yet in the end there was no doubt about the woman's skill.

It didn't take long. She drove both of them with her rapid, well practiced movements. Her body was so skilled and volatile that it simply squeezed about him like a liquid vice.

Johnny totally lost it. Afterward, as he stood and reached for his clothing, he felt there had been something totally mechanical about the woman. It was all staged. No feelings. The way Gloria had made love to him seemed scripted. Merely a sexual act. She watched him dressing without any emotional reaction on her face, other than a vague and calculating smirk.

"That's just a sampling of what I can do to a man…when there's more time. Remember and deliver!"

He left her dressing room, some what dazed. It had been amazingly skillful, yet without any sense of reality. She had drained him like a machine gone wild. Yet her eyes had remained somewhat calculating. Coldly mapping each move to match his obvious reactions to her.

Sexually Gloria had knocked him silly! Emotionally she left him cold.

* * * * * * *

Johnny drove through Hollywood, then down Sunset Boulevard. Neither he nor Jean had said much since she'd gotten into the car. Finally she broke the silence.

"Where are you taking me?"

"I don't know. Have any objections?"

"No. I guess not."

Silence followed for another few miles, until they were entering Beverly Hills, driving along the quiet darkened street, the green of trees and shrubbery surrounding them.

"What happened between you and Gloria?" Jean finally asked, taking a cigarette from her purse.

"Nothing."

She lighted the cigarette, let smoke trail slowly from her full lips. "That's not what I heard, Johnny."

"Jack!"

"Okay. What's this you have on this Johnny bit?"

"My ex-wife called me that!"

"Oh. I didn't know you were married."

"Not for long. It's a dirty story—and I don't like talking about dirty stories!"

"Oh." The word was thoughtful, slightly puzzled.

"Gloria said she had it made with you," Jean announced bitterly. "Is that true?"

"No.

"What made her say it then?" The edge of cattiness to her voice annoyed him.

"I don't know," he lied.

"Yes you do, Jack. You know. I know. Gloria is

a little slut. She'd climb into bed with any man. And when she wants something, she can turn on the sex real hard!"

"So, what's your complaint?" He had to force down the finish to the thought: you aren't so clean yourself. He felt suddenly cheap even having thought that about Jean. Even though he realized she had spread for the cameras, there was something about Jean that caused him to try to excuse her movie-acting career. That annoyed him, too.

"I'm sorry, Jack. Maybe we shouldn't have gotten together tonight."

"Now what does that mean?" Johnny looked at her.

"Oh—forget it. We were supposed to start all over. Introduction. I'm Jean."

"I'm Jack." He laughed. The annoyance melted slightly. He felt a certain closeness to Jean. Maybe it was because she had a sense of values, even though her experience in the stag movie business was far from morally clean. It was something under the surface of her personality, her wanting to be respected, that appealed to him. He was a dirty son of a bitch, too. Silence. Then: "Hungry, Jean?"

"Starved. I know a place in Santa Monica."

Twenty minutes later they were sitting over hamburgers and hot coffee.

It was strange, but he felt as if he had known her for a very long time. There was very little awkwardness. He felt comfortable with her. And that didn't really make much sense. Yet, at the same time, it was like a first date. Strangely so.

Looking at Jean across the small restaurant table, Johnny was almost able to convince himself that she was some girl he'd met at school, and they were having their little snack after a movie. She had a little-girl look about her, a personality vibration that made it easy to forget what she was.

"Tell me something about yourself, Jean," Johnny suggested as he pushed aside his empty plate and pulled the coffee closer.

"What's there to know? I came from a small town. I won a beauty contest, was contacted by a Hollywood talent scout. After a screen test, Galactic Productions signed me to a six-month deal, and then dropped the option when my time was up. I'd been pressed into several little couches and a couple of roles. I felt dirty and cheap. After that I worked as a cocktail waitress. Lived alone and got lonely. Met a real no-good bastard that got me pregnant, and..." Her voice trailed off. A blush colored her cheeks. "What the hell am I telling you all this for?"

"Because I'm really interested." He gazed intensely into her eyes, wanting to communicate how much he was interested. "Please..."

She sat there, staring back and for a long time it seemed as if they were somehow connected in a deep sense.

"If you don't want to..." Johnny started to say, but his voice faded there.

"What...difference does it really make?" she wondered, more to herself than to him.

After a moment, Jean managed to decide to continue. "Gone this far, might as well tell you the rest of the dirt." She finished off her hamburger and then stirred cream and sugar into her coffee. "It's not a nice story, Jack!"

"Go on."

112

"The bastard wanted out, quick, and introduced me to your dear, sweet uncle. Ben Henderson has contacts all over the place."

Johnny couldn't hold back his amazement "You mean he arranged things for—what? An adoption, abortion?"

"He fixed things up real sweet. Said if I did a few favors for him, he'd see to it that things were fixed up. I'd get my abortion. The movie—the first one—was my payment."

Johnny felt sudden emotion choked up through his stomach; a hate he'd never known was possible to feel. What kind of man was Ben Henderson?

"Let's get the hell out of here!" he choked, picking up the check

Once in the car, they sat there while Jean finished her story.

"After the first film, he used it to force me into doing another—with the promise of letting me do something a little more legitimate." She hesitated and studied Johnny. "You don't seem to mind my saying things about your uncle."

"Why should I? I hardly know Ben Henderson. And the more I learn about him, the more I dislike his guts!"

"He's a real cute operator, Johnny."

Johnny tensed, started to correct her about his name, then decided against it. "Why don't you get out—while you can? You know he'll just use the picture thing as a wedge to make you hop."

Jean shrugged. "If I left, Ben would merely see to it that people learned about me—people who might give me jobs. Or if I ran home, he'd make things impossible. I told you he's a dirty man." Her

113

voice was bitter. "Oh, let's not talk about it! There's nothing I can do about it—nothing at all. So the only thing left is hope for the best." She looked into Johnny's eyes. "Do you understand what I'm saying?"

Johnny felt a tenderness sweep over him. He slid his arm around her shoulder and then pulled her gently to him. Their lips met for a short moment and then she gently drew away.

"Not here; Johnny. Not now."

Strangely there was no hesitation about their mutual desire. There was no element of game-playing, merely a simple uncomplicated need for one another: two adults beyond child-games, demanding nothing beyond the moment.

Without another word, Johnny started the engine and drove down Wilshire Boulevard. When they came in sight of a motel, he slowed the car.

"In there?"

She murmured, "Yes."

Then Johnny remembered he didn't have any real hard cash on him.

"Can I borrow some money?" he asked, pulling into the parking lot.

Jean laughed. "That's a new line. Bring a girl into a motel, and let her pay the way."

"I didn't remember!" he snapped angrily, whipping around toward her.

"Hold on, man. I was just kidding." Her lips pecked his nose. "Here, this should take care of it.

He took the money.

Fifteen minutes later they were inside a small motel room. Jean sat down on the bed, staring up at him.

Johnny felt a sense of uneasiness. It bothered him having to borrow the money from Jean. And that didn't make sense, considering how many times he'd lived off broads. But that had been different—they were rich little bitches, more than willing to pay out for a young stud that could give them a thrill. He didn't like the life he'd lived, but after what his wife's family had done to him, he had needed to get back at their kind. Johnny realized how childish his attitude had been.

Shrugging the thoughts off, he focused his attention on Jean. She was lovely.

They stood there awkwardly for a long time, without saying anything.

Johnny suddenly realized that he was more tired than he'd known. The bed looked more inviting than he liked to admit. Shrugging, he stepped over to Jean. He sat down beside her and leaned her back onto the bed.

A faint stir of desire awakened in him as he took in the loveliness of her. Remembering how she'd looked in the stag movie sparked an intense need to see her body naked to his kisses.

Slowly he caressed up under her skirt, feeling for the soft flesh above her stocking.

She writhed slightly and then smiled up at him. "That feels good, Johnny."

"It's supposed to."

"Take off my clothes."

Carefully, taking his time, Johnny began caressing her legs, slipping her skirt upward over her thighs and then unclasping the stockings from her garters. Working her stocking off each soft, firm leg, he felt the beginning of desire start to send

115

strength through him. The idea of sleeping faded far away.

He ran his fingers up her thigh and across the soft expanse of her hips. She lay there quietly, eyes closed, waiting.

Finally his hands slipped under her back and unclasped the white bra. Her breasts were firm and soft, still holding their shape even though she was on her back.

Looking down at Jean's naked body, Johnny remembered what she had told him of the past, of the way men had used her body, taken advantage of her. He felt inwardly angry at those nameless men— including his uncle. Jean was so childlike, so helpless looking.

Slowly he leaned over her and cupped a breast in his hand and his lips folded over the red point of her nipple.

Jean writhed, her hand caressing his shoulder.

"Oh, Johnny—Johnny!" Her hands clutched each shoulder, drawing him into the delicate softness of her breasts.

For a long time he kissed her breasts, and then moved downward into the soft, flat expanse of her white stomach. Desire drove him into the warmth of her hips, kissing, caressing. Then suddenly he stood, stripped off his clothing, and moved down to Jean who surged hungrily to him. There was little buildup, yet neither seemed in a hurry. They simply enveloped one another in a needy embrace that brought their hips together, locked in fire. That simple. Like one unified body they moved, and the rhythm of their love jarred them against the bed.

Jean clawed wildly to him, her nails digging

116

deep into his buttocks, drawing him tighter to her. His movements became more and more subtle, more lingering and more controlled as he drove deeply into her heated lips of love. The soft moans became hard, agonized gasps as the tense rhythm built, driving them more and more violently against one another.

Finally, when he couldn't stand it any longer, he felt her strain up convulsively against him. Then colors burst sensation throughout his whole being.

After that came utter, complete, exhausted sleep.

CHAPTER EIGHT

The next days were a series of half shadows to Johnny. He managed to stay away from Laura, even though the woman made every attempt she could to get him alone.

The nights at the club were a torture. Gloria kept throwing her breasts at him at every chance. Jean kept quietly attempting to take him over completely. That second night he took Jean to her apartment and they made love, finding a joy and excitement that surprised him.

Each night for a week he managed to keep away from Gloria, and let Jean take over. But every night with Jean drew a deeper feeling from him, a complete exhaustion of pleasure and emotional satisfaction. During the days he kept thinking more and more about Jean, and was annoyed by the fact.

Laura had finally grown silent when he was around, but the way her eyes kept following every action he made was unnerving.

It was as much his need for escape from Laura's watchful eyes as it was his need for Jean's body that drove him toward the cocktail waitress.

One night a customer got fresh with Jean and he had to step in the way, cooling the man off. Alone that night, Jean was all over him with frantic love-making. Her body hungrily folded around him, the soft warmth of her encasing him in hot fire.

And the next morning, when he returned to the Henderson home, Laura was there to look at him, silently revealing her jealousy.

Then one night, after having been at the club for a week, Gloria managed to trap Johnny at the bar.

"How about us cutting out after closing time?" she suggested. "I want to talk over a few things with you."

"You know how it is, Gloria," he countered, hoping he wouldn't be forced into being rude to her.

"You've put me off long enough, Jack." Her breast pressed into his shoulder, then withdrew. The suggestion was obvious.

Johnny considered. He looked at the large thrust of her breasts. Gloria wanted raw sex; nothing more. No emotional tangles. She knew what she was, and didn't try to claim otherwise. She lived on the sensual side of life with an intense hunger. Memory of their quick, one-shot session that first night at the club caused a tingling sensation to run through him.

"Come on, lover," Gloria cooed. Her breast pressed suggestively into his arm again. "I'll show you things you've never heard about."

Just then Jean stepped up, wedging herself between them.

"Have anything planned for tonight, Johnny?" she asked. The expression on her face was open jealousy. "I thought we might go over to my place for a snack." Her voice was just loud enough so that Gloria could hear.

Johnny caught Gloria's eyes, held for a moment,

then he looked at Jean.

Gloria was nothing but raw sex. Intriguing in a strangely erotic way; nothing more.

Jean was something special; and a bit frightening. He wanted to feel the softness of her.

"Sure, honey. Sure."

When Jean was gone, Gloria looked stonily at him. "What's this?"

"Private—if you know what I mean."

She was silent for a moment. Then, "You give me equal time, and you won't want that little lush!"

"Shut up, Gloria—just shut up!" he demanded, angered. "You don't have any rights—period."

For a moment he thought she was going to explode. But instead she merely shrugged and smiled. "What happened before in my dressing room was nothing to what you'll enjoy...when I give you a full course, without any time limit. You'll never want another woman after that. Believe me. I'll just wait, lover—just wait."

Johnny watched her wiggle away from him. And at the sight of her hips, jerking with every step, he knew that she wouldn't have to wait long. And he couldn't help wonder what she might offer that so many other women hadn't. Yet the action of her holding him inside her had been amazing.

He forgot all about Gloria once she was out of sight. His thoughts surrendered to the images of Jean. He looked forward to being with her.

That night something happened that Johnny hadn't expected.

After he ate a night-lunch of scrambled eggs, minute steak, and a couple of homemade martinis, Jean stood and silently invited him into her bedroom. There they quickly undressed and settled on the bed.

They just lay there for a long time, holding each other, feeling a restful relaxation at their intimate nearness.

Jean was first to break the silence.

"What's between you and Gloria?" Her voice was neither jealous nor worried.

"Nothing, really, Jean. She wants to get into those porno pics, like I told you. She wants to get me alone, some quiet place, and give me an all-night session to make sure that I do everything I can to help her."

"That's all?" She raised an eyebrow.

Johnny laughed, doubling over.

"It's enough," he assured her after gaining control of himself.

"You like her?" Jean inquired, reaching out and caressing him.

He looked into her eyes and for a moment felt an emotion that he'd never felt for a woman. It irritated him. He liked Jean too much for his own good.

He reached for Jean, crushing her body to him.

For some time they kissed each other, completely exploring each other's mouths.

Then he slid his lips along the soft white of her throat, down over her shoulder and then into the fullness of her breasts.

Jean trembled and dug her hands into his arms.

And with every caress and kiss, he felt a gripping inside his chest, a tenderness, a lonely ache that reached out to enfold Jean in his emotions. It was a feeling that excited, and at the same time annoyed.

He didn't want to feel anything but passion for

this woman. He'd wanted to lay her merely because she was easy, quick, and he knew her—nothing more. Or so he'd been sure. Suddenly he began to doubt it.

Jean urged his head down lower, across her stomach and then between her thighs. As his kisses became more intimate, she gasped and strained against him, sobbing.

He wanted to give her pleasure more than he'd ever given another woman; he wanted to make her scream with need for him. He wanted to take his time. He could feel her nails cut at his skin, and the excitement and thrill of that fact overwhelmed him. Then suddenly he wasn't able to hold off any longer and was enveloped in such pleasure that all he could think of were the wild, collective sensations racing through him.

A little later they both sat up in bed, staring at each other.

"God, Johnny, I never—never had anything like it!" she exhaled in a weak, breathless voice. She hugged him and then withdrew. Standing, she left the room and a few minutes later returned with drinks and cigarettes.

"All the comforts of home!" she laughed, plopping down beside him.

He put a gentle hand on her thigh, caressing.

"I don't know what happened," he said in a puzzled voice, more to himself than to Jean.

"I do!" she exclaimed happily.

Johnny smiled, but it was *a* forced action of his lips. His mind was stripped bare and raw from the tormenting thoughts racing through him.

Something was happening. Something that he

didn't like at all. He looked at Jean.

She was lovely in the dim lighting of the room. Her breasts were smooth and white, two ovals of satin flesh, the nipples erect, pointing, giving their shape the final artistic touch to make them perfect. Her waist was narrow, flaring out at the hips in rounded circles, then tapering down to lush, firm thighs. Her face was innocent, wide-eyed, her mouth bright with happiness.

But she had made those films. The reasons didn't change that fact. It was cheap, dirty, and made her the property of any man, woman or child who might see them.

How could a man feel anything other than sexual desire for the woman on the screen—or the woman in the flesh? She had cheapened herself.

Yet Johnny felt an emotional response toward Jean. During those moments when their bodies were insanely joined, when she was encasing him in her, he had felt sensations that were of the mind, not merely of the body. He'd wanted to give to her—not take. And that was the first sign of love.

Irritably Johnny took the drink she was still holding for him, and gulped it down. Standing, he asked, "Where's some more of that?"

Jean frowned and then nodded into the living room.

"Kitchen. Help yourself."

Johnny returned a few moments later with a water glass filled with martini.

Jean's mouth dropped, amazement widened her eyes. "That much will kill you!"

Johnny laughed, but it wasn't humor. He wanted to die, mentally, for the next hours. He didn't want to think about the emotional response that had attached him while a part of Jean's warm body. He wanted only to feel the sensual pleasure, to take that physical offering, and nothing else.

As he sat down next to Jean, the drinks suddenly hit his head, numbing all mental sensation. His eyes focused on one of her breasts.

"Oh, I love you, Johnny—I can't help it, I love you! I love you," she moaned, clutching to him. "Forgive me—I love you!"

And Johnny suddenly he realized his own feelings were approaching the same emotion. Logical or not, sane or not, there was something about the two of them that had clicked that first night, that first time they had been in the same room with one another.

It was later, much later, when he was lying on his back in the darkness, Jean half asleep beside him, that Johnny realized that he would have to stop seeing her. He didn't want serious involvement. The very idea was terrorizing. Casual sex was one thing, making use of a rich woman for the easy life, another, but emotional tangles was something he simply didn't need.

If things continued, he would only end up hurting Jean. And he didn't want to do that; it was the last thing in the world he wanted to do.

Why he should care was even more frightening. They had to be at arms length from one another.

Raw sex and nothing more with some hot chick was all he could afford.

He thought about Gloria Sparks, who was the logical fun and games girl. Laura was dangerously off-limits, and Jean an emotional trap. He needed to break it off with her before it was too late to do so gracefully.

Johnny slipped from the bed and gathered up his clothing.

Jean sat up and stared at him.

"What are you doing?" she asked in an alarmed voice.

"Going—getting out of here!" he told her in a harsh voice.

She stood, rushed to him. Her arms slid around his neck. "What's wrong, Johnny?"

"And don't call me Johnny!" he snapped nastily. Sickness clawed his throat. He hated being nasty to her.

But it was the only way

"Oh God, what have I done?" She clutched at him. Gently but firmly Johnny pushed her away from him holding her at arm's length, "Jean—I'm sorry!"

Her eyes moistened. Even in the darkness he could see the tears glistening on her cheeks

"It's what I told you, isn't it? How I felt about you—and what I am. It isn't."

Johnny forced the words out, choking on them. "Yes—it is. There's nothing for us, and you know it."

The turned and moved to the bed.

For a moment Johnny stood there, fighting to keep from going to her and folding her into his arms. There was a tight lump in his throat and a be-ginning of moisture in his eyes. *Goddam, you're cursed.* Stepping forward, Johnny pulled Jean into his arms.

"Look, honey, don't take it so hard. It's just that

I'm not the kind of guy for you. And—"

"Screw you, Johnny Belton. Screw you!" she cursed, pushing him away. Her hand whipped out across his face. "You goddamned bastard. Get out of here. Don't ever let me see you again. Never again!"

"Thanks," Johnny managed to say, holding down the inner fury. "Thanks—that makes it easier!"

With that he walked out of the apartment.

He didn't drive directly back to the Henderson home It was light by the time he turned his car back toward Los Angeles. He had driven up the coast highway, far beyond Ventura. The mental battle he'd fought had exhausted him. By the time he reached Santa Monica, his eyes were blurry and it was almost impossible to keep them open. Finding a motel, he parked the car. A few minutes later he was lying in a double bed, sound asleep.

CHAPTER NINE

That night Johnny attempted to keep as far away from Jean as possible. She seemed occupied by the same desire for distance. They hardly saw each other. He sat at the far end of the bar, away from the cocktail waitress station.

As the evening progressed through one strip after another, Johnny managed to keep his eyes on Gloria Spark's show and ignore the rest.

The idea of shacking up with the broad had an effect on him. His nerves were shattered from the realization of how he had begun to feel about Jean; he needed another woman to take the bite of emotional agony from him. That afternoon he'd searched Hollywood for an apartment and finally picked a furnished one with a bedroom and home bar. He planned on moving in the next day. Laura had been silent about his plans, but the look in her eyes had puzzled him; it was amused, intensely interested. Ben Henderson had shrugged the announcement off with a warning to keep clean of any complications with broads. "Get one in trouble, let me know—I'll fix it up!"

It was well past twelve before Gloria stepped out from the back stage. He was seated just outside

127

the curtained doorway, and when she started past, he called out her name.

The stony look that Gloria gave him as she turned at his call surprised Johnny.

"What's wrong, baby?" he asked, standing and walking to her.

Her eyes lighted. "Style changing?"

Her breasts pressed against him.

"Changing style," Johnny admitted, letting his eyes follow her dipping neckline. An animal charge whipped through him like the thrust of a rapier.

"Honey, that's what I've been waiting for." She hesitated, then asked, "What's happened between you and that little bar girl?"

Johnny tensed, frowned at her reference to Jean. "None of your business, honey."

She shrugged off the remark and then patted his cheek. "Wait for me, lover, after work. I'll take you to my pad. You'll have the show of your life—a promise!"

With that, she twisted away from him.

He sat there for the rest of the evening, until Carter called him in to help count the night's receipts. His mind kept telling him that Gloria was going to be very good after what had happened the night before. Raw, naked, down and dirty sex. But his emotions kept fighting the mental argument. Every time he caught sight of Jean Harold, he kept remembering the deep, overwhelming feeling that had attacked him the night before; the sudden realization that he might be falling in love with the woman was simply impossible.

Annoyed, Johnny had managed to have several strong drinks, and by the time he went into Carter's office, he was high.

"You better lay off the booze, Jack," Carter warned.

"You better lay off me!" Johnny warned back.

Carter frowned and then his lips spread wide. "Sorry, didn't mean anything—"

"Calm down your windpipe. Just because Uncle Ben is—"

"Okay, Jack. Forget it. Just that I was giving you a friendly warning." A little later he said, "Hear you're cutting out with Gloria."

"So?"

"Well, you know how I feel about her?"

"No," Johnny admitted. He'd forgotten his uncle's warning.

"I don't like it, Jack." The man's face was quite serious; controlled.

"That's too bad, Carter. I think it's Gloria's business who she goes out with. She's been on my back for days now. If you can't keep her happy or her promises to her—" The expression on the other man's face cut him short. Johnny tensed, ready for an attack.

"Okay—I'll take it up with her." Then Carter shrugged. "Doesn't matter, anyway. Just as long as nothing serious develops. I like her—and she's a good lay."

Johnny felt annoyed, but held down the retort that tickled his tongue.

By 2:20 he stepped into the club. Gloria wasn't there. He went into the back and found her in her dressing room.

"Well, come on, Gloria," he told her, holding the door wide open. "What's keeping you?"

She grinned and stood, turning to face him. "Just finishing touches."

A moment later they were getting into his Ford. She gave instructions to her place. She lived in West Los Angeles, on the border of Santa Monica.

Her apartment was extremely quaint, considering the type of work she did. It was home, with worn furnishings. There was one luxury in the corner of the room—a hi-fi set.

She kicked off her shoes and wiggled across the living room and into the kitchen.

"What'll you have, lover?"

"What you got?"

Johnny followed her into the kitchen. She was standing at the cupboard. She looked ridiculously out of place in the kitchen. Her huge, voluptuous body was tightly pressed into the too-small dress that clung to her; it just didn't fit in with a domestic setting. Johnny found it hard to keep from laughing.

She opened the cupboard, revealing a large display of booze.

"Anything you want, lover." She turned, grinning at him. "For a big girl like me, you're something of a fascinating man."

"Now what does that mean?" he demanded defensively.

"Well, I am a little on the large size for you, aren't I?" She giggled. "Breasts over you!"

"Shut up and fix a strong scotch!" Johnny demanded.

She mixed scotch and soda in tall glasses. She walked to him and thrust her hips against his, her breasts flush to his chest. "Lover, you're in for one helluva ball! And…in the end it'll all me mine!"

130

They went into the living room. Gloria turned on the hi-fi set and then sat down beside him on the sofa.

"You have a spat with your little girl?" she asked seriously.

"How's that?" Johnny felt surprise choke the words down his throat.

"Well, you've been cooling it with me ever since that first night. I'd begun to think you weren't interested in me anymore. With the other girl—what's her, name, Jean something or other—I thought it was beginning to get serious."

"Who gets serious with a girl like her?" Johnny asked, both irritated by her questions and by the fact that what she had said had to be true. But he wondered if it was already too late.

"Guys like you!"

"What's that mean?"

"Well, you men are all the same in some ways. A girl like me, well, I'm just fun and games. Girls like her...well, she gets a man all screwed up in her vulnerability. Makes him feel protective and all that. Me?

"Well, I'm what you see...you get. I love the stage. I like stripping for a man. I enjoy him getting all excited over my body. I like turning a man on, full charge. I really don't want much more. I'm hot at getting him ready for my final act."

"What's that?"

"Oh. That's the Forbidden Temple of Love!"

"Sounds intriguing."

"I'll show a few rooms tonight!"

"Where is it located?" he chuckled.

"Where do you think?"

131

His eyes flowed to her hips and then linger a bit lower. "Somewhere down there?"

"Something like that, honey."

"You showed me that in your dressing room. Remember?"

"Naughty boy! You were just given a little peep show. Tonight you get a lot more! A full length feature!" Gloria laughed and reached down between his legs, and laughed again, withdrawing her hand.

"Honey I love it!" She giggled. "Big, juicy man!"

"You should know!" Johnny countered, gulping his drink.

They were silent for a moment and then Gloria stood, went to the hi-fl set, flipped through several records, picked one out and put it on

The music that suddenly blared from the speakers was wild rhythm. She turned and looked at Johnny. The smile and expression on her big face were pure sensual heat, wild and savage. "I'll give you a real hot one tonight! A Catch the Kitten in the Temple of Love!"

"What the hell does that mean?"

"Oh, you'll see. Soon you'll be saying to me 'here pussy, pussy, come to daddy!'" She laughed broadly. "Get it?"

"Well, I hope you give it to me."

"Depends on what you have for the little kitten! She likes her meat real raw and wild like! She'll gobble that up, ravish it between her hungry lips! You'd be amazed what my little kitty can do to the right kind of meal! Devour it whole! So enjoy the show, honey!"

Johnny laughed, now feeling suddenly quite

132

comfortable with this woman. She might be raw, but certainly offered an inviting show. He could only guess at what was going to happen. This might be just what he needed!

Gloria's wide hips started circling with the music. She raised her arms high above her head, and the soft, supple mountains of her breasts rose in response. It was the first time he noticed she didn't wear a bra.

"No bra!" Johnny observed.

"Never—except on the stage. Don't need them. Every muscle is kept in tone, in shape by exercises," she announced, jerking her hips into a circular motion.

"You like my body, Jack?" she murmured, blowing him a very un-stagy kiss. "Does it make you want to let the kitty have its way with you?"

"What do you think?"

Gloria laughed and lost the rhythm of the music. Recovering, her arms went around to the back of her dress and slowly, teasingly, she started unzipping it. Then, with a mocking grin, she lowered the top of her dress to reveal the smooth expanse of one breast all the way to her oversize nipple. Then she covered it up. "Wanna suck titties? Or something hotter?"

Johnny watched her go through the slow, teasing routine of revealing her breasts and finally lowering the dress to her waist, all the time jerking and bumping to the music. He wondered what could possess her to want to do a stag movie[9] Surely not publicity or money She made a mint according to his uncle The only logical reason he could think of was for kicks, thrills.

Johnny's mind wandered strangely, during her

dance, even though his eyes watched every movement of her large, voluptuous body.

He thought about the other women he d had in the past, the long exercise of living off rich dames and the cheap way he'd felt about all that. It wasn't until Gloria was completely naked, standing there before him, whipping her body in excited grinding motions, that his mind snapped back to her. Her large breasts bobbed and swayed almost within reach.

Her hips jerked forward, circled and then trembled, as a delighted little cry broke from her lips. The expression on her face was pure animal sex. It looked as if she were getting her orgasm right then.

Bending low, her hips started the little jerking movements that strippers were famous for, except she didn't have anything on, which added a lot to the show. Her eyes were frozen to his, and the burning heat in them was almost laughable. She stood, thrust her hips forward and repeated her jerking movements. The blood was throbbing at his temples. His hands were shaking.

Standing, Johnny found himself quickly, frantically stripping.

Gloria laughed in delight when she saw his naked body.

"Is that all for me?" she moaned in delight, a beefy thigh pressing against him.

The tip of her tongue ran along his lips, then between them, probing deep as she reached around and gripped at his buttocks.

As her tongue withdrew, she murmured: "Oh… my kitten wants to devour you!"

She moaned, dropped to her knees before him.

134

All at once, as if totally out of her mind, she enveloped him, head whipping wildly from side to side.

Just as quickly, Gloria stopped, releasing him.

Standing, she bent backward until her body became a total arch, thighs spread wide, hands over her head, resting on the floor behind her.

"Do me, now!" she cried.

Her hips wiggled, legs parted wider.

Laughing throatily, Johnny pressed against her.

Slowly she rose, while he held her hips in his hands. She came to a standing position, still embracing him deep within her. Those wide, fleshy hips started rotating and moving rapidly, driving insane pleasure through him. Johnny lost total control and giggled in delight.

With that, Gloria led him to the sofa.

It was like being taken by a storm. He couldn't refuse her hot, erotic demands.

The rhythm of their bodies strained perfectly together as they moved with an almost animal beauty. It was a ballet of love. A savage, animal dance.

Then suddenly stars burst before his eyes, explosions took place, and then they were slipping away from each other.

Johnny stood and looked down at the exhausted woman Her huge body was relaxed, her eyes closed.

An inner disgust choked in Johnny's throat. It had been great, the excitement and pleasure of their bodies joined in the action of sexual union, but there had been a degenerate thing about it that sickened.

Johnny suddenly knew what was bothering him, and the realization sent a shudder through him.

After Jean, sex with a woman, without that emotional attachment, was merely a mechanical thing with little meaning.

Johnny felt sudden anger. All he wanted to do was run and never stop running.

The world had all at once become insane, upside down, irrational.

CHAPTER TEN

Gloria stirred, looked up at him, grinned: "You're good, lover. Good!"

She reached for him, but he stepped away.

"What's wrong, lover—all pooped? Can't pop any more?"

He cursed under his breath and then shook his head. "Give me some booze, and then we escape right into the bedroom!"

Minutes later he was gulping raw whiskey. It took a little while for it to affect him. He waited. Gloria had disappeared into the bedroom and was waiting for him.

An inner anguish tore through him.

What a paradox is life had become. *You run from the sticks and chicks with money, right into another trap. It didn't make sense; it wasn't sane.*

And now you want to run again, and never stop running. Yet that's why you came to Hollywood. To stop running.

Johnny poured himself another drink.

He didn't want to think; he didn't want to consider the wild implications of what was happening.

The liquor soothed his nerves, racing through his blood.

He finished off the last of the whiskey in the glass, refilled it and turned toward the bedroom. He found Gloria stretched out on the bed, her legs ready for him. She opened her arms as he slid down into the largeness of her breasts.

Johnny mothered himself against her supple mountains. She pressed up against his face and her hand held his head against her. "That's it, baby, mommy wants you to do it like that."

Where now, little man, he wondered. More escaping from life? More running until there isn't any place to run?

Gloria pressed him down over her stomach then shifted, turned, twisted; then her lips found him.

The endless nightmare escape into the lush rhythm of the woman's body merged over all thought until exhaustion left him spent. Darkness clouded over Johnny as he fell into a deep sleep. He didn't awaken until late the next morning. Gloria was still sleeping as he got up from bed. Ten minutes later he was sitting in his car, driving toward Beverly Hills.

As he drove, fighting the hangover that pounded in his brain, and he felt drained and slightly disgusted at how things had been developing. He wanted Jean so badly that his whole being ached with the wanting. This was all too new to him.

When he got to the Henderson home it was close to twelve. He went up the balcony directly to his room. He was in the process of packing when a knock sounded on his door.

"Yes?"

"Laura."

Johnny tensed. "What do you want?"

"Can I come in?" Her voice was almost pleading.

He considered, then realized there was nothing else to do but let her in. The last time she'd been in the bedroom with him, they'd made quite a night of it.

"Okay—come on in," he called, slamming his suitcase on the bed. The door opened and Laura stepped in, closing it after her. She stood against the door. A robe was pulled around her body, and from the way it clung to her shape, he knew there was little on underneath.

He tried to ignore her

There was a long silence while he packed. Then Laura said, "Ben's gone on location, Jack."

The meaning was quite obvious. "And I'm leaving for my own apartment. So that aces out that little party idea!"

He still refused to look at her.

Silence. Then, "That shouldn't make any difference, should it?"

Johnny turned and stared at Laura. His face was set hard he tightened the hard muscles of his stomach forcing himself to ignore the lush beauty of this woman.

"No! No, Laura. No. I told you it was finished! And I meant it."

Her face looked as if it were about to crumble. "Jack you don't know how it's been. I've gone almost out of my mind. Being in this house with you—knowing how good it was with us—and having Ben touch me and make love to me and never even start to satisfy me…I need you, Jack! Oh God—I wish I'd never met you. Things were simple before you came. I found ways to—" She hesitated then swallowed hard. "There were other men—I guess you knew that."

"I guess I guessed it," Johnny admitted. "So go back to your other lovers."

"I can't. I tried. But I need you, Jack!" She rushed forward, throwing her arms around his neck. The pressure of her body against his, soft, yielding, proved beyond doubt that she was completely naked under the robe. "I've been waiting for you to get back. Oh, God, the nights, knowing you were out with another woman, giving her what you gave me—what my body needed so desperately, so terribly."

Her hand reached down and clutched at his groin in such an intimate way that control suddenly crumbled.

His lips crushed against Laura's and then he felt the point of her tongue draw his deep into her mouth.

The embrace lasted just long enough for him to realize what would happened if this wasn't stopped.

He pushed her away. "No, Laura. Just cut it out!"

She stared at him, her eyes streaming with tears. "God, Jack. I'll do anything—"

Johnny merely laughed, but it was a bitter, humorless sound. "Just go, Laura. Before you make a real fool of yourself!"

Suddenly, without warning, she slapped his face. It was a stinging blow.

It took all the control and strength left to Johnny to keep from slapping her back. Breaking into a sweat, he pushed her toward the door.

Without a word he opened the door and shoving her out.

Strangely enough he woman hadn't even resisted, but simply rushed down the hall. He closed the door and returned to packing his clothing and then went to the balcony, down the steps and to his car.

Johnny sat in the car for some time trying to gain control over his shaking nerves.

The scene with Laura had left him exhausted. Several months before he might not have refused a woman in such a situation. Hollywood had already placed its mark on him; he'd changed. And he didn't know if he liked the change. He knew that if she ever tried anything like that again, he might not be able to turn her down.

Shaking his head, he started the engine and drove down the street.

That night, at the club, Johnny found it impossible not to watch Jean Harold. And with every glance her way, the inner ache burst inside him. He didn't want to care about her, but he couldn't help it. Regardless of what his uncle had told him about Jean, he couldn't help feeling she was special. There was a difference between an all-out tramp and Jean. In that way she was exactly like himself.

Gloria came up to him and sat down at the bar. "What happened?"

"What are you talking about?" he demanded irritably.

"You split."

"Just wanted to be alone."

"How about tonight?" She kissed his ear and cheek, her breasts pressing his arm.

He wanted to tell her to go to hell.

"My place?" she invited.

Just then Jean happened to pass by them, and her eyes met his. It was the look in her eyes that decided him. She was searching, pleading, calling out for his love and affection and attention.

"Okay, honey, we can go to my place," he said, loudly enough so that Jean could hear.

The hurt, almost frantic expression in Jean's eyes stabbed Johnny with a terrible responding pain.

He was half loaded by closing time.

Carter, in his office, while they were counting the night's receipts, asked Johnny for his new address.

"How'd you know about my moving?"

"News gets around. Gotta have your address and phone number just in case something comes up."

"No phone yet, but I'll get one." He gave the man his address.

Carter's eyes followed him out of the office and Johnny was aware of the man watching as he greeted Gloria.

That night Gloria was intense, savage, wild; more exploring than the night before.

He was sleeping restfully when a warm, soft body pressed to his. Opening his eyes, Johnny found himself looking into the large point of Gloria's breast.

With a curse, Johnny shoved her away from him.

"What's wrong?" she cried, alarmed.

"A hangover."

She reached for him, circling her arms around his neck; her lips caressed his before he could stop her. "I got something that'll cure what you have!" she murmured, pressing tight against him. "A real hot hungry kitty cat."

Cursing at himself, Johnny shoved Gloria down onto the bed, pinning her arms to her sides.

She moaned and thrust her hips up, searching his. "Lover, lover—you're great"

Just at that point the doorbell rang.

The two of them froze. She looked alarmed. "Who could that be?"

"Damned if I know."

"Don't answer it! Please!" she whispered. "Forget the door!"

"No, I better answer…who knows who it might be."

She sighed. "But get rid of them. Hurry back to me. Please."

A strange, impossible idea that it was Jean Harold standing outside in the hallway coursed through Johnny as he pulled on his robe and tied it around his lean, hard body. '

Closing the bedroom door, he crossed the living room and flung open the front door.

Laura Henderson stood there in a black sheath. She wore white gloves and a small, black hat. Without saying a word, she stepped forward and closed the door behind her.

"Well, big boy, this time you aren't running away. I told you I'd do anything to have you—and I'm going to have you. This time you'll do exactly as I say, no holds barred." Her smile was challenging, while at the very same time triumphant.

Gloria was in the next room and could hear everything that went on.

"Look, Laura, I don't think this is the right time to talk about this, because—"

"Please, Johnny. Please." The control which had kept her face from revealing the deep emotion tight inside her suddenly crumbled. "I feel cheap and dirty, begging. But I know what it was like—I know you liked it with me and I want us to start a real thing…we can have so much fun together. Now that you have this pad we can really have a wonderful fling and nobody will know."

"Not now!" Johnny warned. He looked toward the bedroom.

Laura's face whitened. "Who's in there?"

"Gloria Sparks."

Stunned, Laura managed to crumble into the brown chair behind her.

Johnny started for the bedroom when the door burst open and Gloria stepped out, fully dressed. She looked at Laura and then at Johnny.

"Real cute, lover."

Johnny decided on a bluff. "This is Laura Banks."

Gloria shook her head. "Sorry, lover—but nice try. I've met Mrs. Henderson. Ben brought her in one night to see the show, introduced us around and then left."

Gloria's face was bright with excitement. "Now I think we'll have a little talk. I'll be silent about your little, well, let's call it relationship, if I'm given a major role in one of hubby's films."

Laura merely nodded.

"Now get your ass out of here!" she screamed, standing suddenly. "And you leave Jack alone! That's the deal."

144

Gloria's face hardened. "You can have him… there's a lot of others just like little Johnny-boy around to enjoy my body. I don't need him any more. You just set things up with your hubby or else I'll tell him everything I just learned."

Then she slowly walked out of the apartment.

"Bye, lovers, you deserve one another. Have fun!" she laughed, slamming the door behind her.

"Bitch!" Laura snapped.

Johnny just shrugged, strangely not caring. Gloria had been nothing but a lush body to use as a way to escape other feelings, needs, confusions. Now he had to deal with Laura.

"Well, Jack, looks like she was simply using you!"

"Went both ways!" he shock back as he mixed both of them drinks.

Laura laughed as he handed her a drink. "Boy, you're really something!"

"I'm something, all right!" he snapped, sick at the whole thing.

He studied the woman, she looked uncertain, a bit angry and confused.

That reflected his own mood. His nerves felt like they were falling apart. Things had looked lousy before, because of his personal life, but he'd seen everything going up in smoke, and landing him down right where he'd started. If Gloria blabbed they were all in shit.

Laura, hopefully, had taken care of that. Gloria was getting what she'd been after, and now had a super-charged weapon to make certain things ran her way. So, if she wanted to be a big stag film star, this would be were big break. The whole thing disgusted him.

Suddenly he didn't even know if he cared any more about anything. It was always possible to return to his old gig of playing sex-toy to needy woman. It was a dirty racket, but at least had worked for him up until now.

Maybe all he was good for was servicing rich bitched in heat. A very depressing thought.

By the time Laura had swallowed half of the raw whiskey he'd poured, she seemed calmed down, and looked at him in an amused way. "Well, I guess I put my nose in that one."

"Your problem." Johnny was shaken, though. The idea of Ben Henderson finding out about him and Laura had sent cold chills down his spine. "I can always go back to my old trade."

"Kept man?" Laura laughed bitingly. "You know, it's funny. I came here to threaten to tell Ben that you had sex with me, that you seduced me. I guess it would be useless now."

"Damned right."

Johnny stared at her. Their eyes met for a long time, studying each other.

Then something snapped. He had seen that expression in other women's eyes; women he had used for his own means, women who had wanted him as much as Laura wanted him now—the same expression that had been in Jean's eyes the night before. And the inner hate at what he was. He looked into her eyes and saw all the pain he'd given out all his life, and suddenly he wanted to erase it all, blot it out, to do something to somehow even the score.

What difference did it make who he was servicing? One lady was the same as another. Automatically the old Johnny slipped into control. Laura was a woman who had money, position, power. Maybe things would settle down. As long as he managed to keep things controlled, it might be possible to, at the very least, to milk this deal to the ultimate limits. Right now it was necessary to play the game right into this woman's arms. She was the key. As long as Uncle Ben knew nothing about their little affair, it was to their mutual advantage. Gloria didn't count as a threat at all.

Johnny's own options were limited: slink off to nowhere land and pick up where he had been before coming to California, nor play Laura, Ben and all of them to his advantage.

Even Jean might fit in, somewhere, somehow. It didn't matter much any more.

He felt numb in so many ways. And that was good.

"Come," he finally said, looking at Laura. All he had to do was satisfy her needs.

They were both stuck in a life-style that wasn't easy to escape. It didn't make any difference who was to blame. Change didn't come easy; and life could be hard. She might, in fact, in the end, be his best supporter.

With a tired sigh he pulled Laura into his arms, covering her lips with his. The kiss was long, probing, searching, exhausting.

When their lips parted, Laura hugged close to him. Her body clung like a child's. She needed him, and that was all that mattered. A little girl, helpless in the arms of her lover.

"Oh, Jack—I never knew it could happen this way. You're so young, and yet so old for your age.

Oh, if things were only different. If I weren't married, if I were free. I want you so; need you."

He knew she didn't love him in a real way; he simply represented a need. And it was to his advantage to fill it.

Feeling as though he was being drowned in that bottomless pit unable to escape Johnny slowly led Laura toward the bedroom.

"Oh, Jack, I'm crazy about you!"

Crazy seemed almost the key word. But he was committed to this new set of rules she was defining at the very moment.

Laura like a woman possessed. It didn't make sense. It wasn't even sane. Yet there it was. The woman was obsessively needy. Some how there seemed to be almost a wild madness to her actions—as if she were completely out of control, unable to stop her need from consuming both of them.

As he folded his arms around Laura's naked body a few minutes later he felt almost a sense of fatalistic release. From now on there was no turning back no escape from his final ending.

This time it was brutal taking.

CHAPTER ELEVEN

The next days were hellish insanity. Laura spent most of her time with him. How she managed to explain her absence to her household help, he never knew. At night, when he got to his apartment, she was there, her arms waiting, her mouth hungry, her body a voluptuous thing that devoured him with a gluttony that grew with every meeting. There was little rest, and only when their bodies could take no more, give no more, did they find sleep, only to recapture each other upon waking. Her need for him was so intense that it became frightening.

At the club, he found another torment, another pain, watching Jean Harold.

He would see her and want to reach out, caress her hair, kiss her lovely lips and hug her tenderly to him. His body ached to touch the soft satin of her. And his mind kept screaming over and over again that she was a tramp, a slut who made dirty pictures. And another thought would return, reminding him of how she had been forced into the racket, and the arguments would silently continue raging.

Johnny almost looked forward to his hours with Laura. Her hunger enveloped his full attention, drawing all thought and awareness

149

Then on the sixth night he came home and found the apartment empty. He didn't know whether to be relieved or frightened.

Ben Henderson was obviously back.

He paced the apartment, smoking. Then he helped himself to a generous drink, stripped and went to his bedroom. The whiskey fired his nerves, rather than relaxing them. He kept thinking of the wild passion that Laura's body had offered him; the only straw to his sanity. And he thought about the need, emotionally and spiritually, for Jean Harold.

He didn't sleep much. It wasn't until the sun was creeping over the eastern horizon that consciousness finally slipped. Sleep was restless and short. By eleven he was in the kitchen, pouring himself another drink. A little later he took an icy shower. It didn't help. The rest of the afternoon he spent on the beach, alone, away from the popular sections where other people went.

It was there that he realized that it wouldn't be possible to continue long without facing his emotional need for Jean. He couldn't escape forever; he couldn't keep running. That was one of the major reasons for having come to California—to stop running, to find roots and face himself and his life.

Jean had become a part of him, emotionally. One thing he'd learned years before was: avoiding a woman only made her more desirable.

Driving back to his apartment, Johnny came to the only conclusion possible: he would face Jean, head on. It was either that or run. He was through running.

It was a simple thing to arrange. He merely told Jean they had to talk after work. Once he was finished closing the club, she was waiting form him at the bar.

As they walked out of the club, the mental images of Laura and Gloria flashed before his mind. That was another thing he had to deal with; but first his relationship with Jean was all that mattered at this time.

He headed for his apartment. They were silent until he the car in his garage.

"I didn't know you had a place of your own," Jean said. "Getting up in the world!"

Her voice was light, but the words were biting.

His head jerked forward.

"I'm sorry, Jack. That was nasty."

Johnny managed a shrug, smiled and patted Jean on the arm. "Forget it. We can always start over with the name bit."

Both of them laughed then. The tension broke.

"I shouldn't, after the way you treated me, Jack," she told him. "I shouldn't ever talk to you again. I didn't want to. But I've thought a lot—maybe too much. And maybe I don't have the right. Any rights." Her eyes lowered, away from his.

"Forget it."

He got out of the car and a moment later the two of them were entering his apartment.

He mixed the drinks and they sat on the sofa.

"I don't know what's happened," Johnny said. "I don't know if I like it, either. But..." He suddenly, impulsively reached for Jean who simply melted in his arms. The hunger and desperation of her kiss was more exciting than he would have guessed.

As they broke away, Jean looked at him. There was a strange questioning expression in her blue eyes.

"What is it you want, Jack?" she inquired in a shaken voice. She nervously lighted a cigarette.

"What kind of question is that?"

"You know what I mean. After our quick, hot romance, and the blowup, now this—what do you expect a girl to think? You really slammed it down hard on me. I was getting a little emotionally involved with you." Her voice was impersonal, almost businesslike.

"Quite frankly, Jean, you've unnerved me right from the start. At first, well, that first few hours before the film, I thought you were easily pegged."

"Do we have to go back there?" she inquired, bitterly.

"I don't know. But at I need to say this. That film—"

"You were sickened?" she asked harshly.

"Shaken."

Suddenly the tight control that had hardened her words and actions slipped away. Her face seemed to tremble, the muscles fighting against themselves. "I...I don't know what's going to happen to us!" she choked out, all at once crumbling against him. Her arms circled his neck. "Now this. I need you so much, Jack. And I know what I am, what I let myself be conned into doing. People like you and Henderson...look at a girl like me and shrug us aside with contempt."

She pulled away, staring into his eyes. "1 don't want you to think that about me."

"I don't know what to think," Johnny admitted honestly. He caressed her cheek and then kissed her nose. "I know what I feel, and I don't want to feel it.

152

I can't help that, either."

He took a sip of his drink.

They were quiet for a long time, then Jean sighed. "If you want the truth, I want to run, Jack. Run all the way, and never look back. But I can't. Your uncle has a hold on me, and I can't break away. He's a degenerate man, Jack. A real no-good son of a bitch!"

She looked at him suddenly; her face was hard and bitter. "You know, I wanted to get into the movies—at first. Now I don't want that any more. I want respectability. I want a home and family. I want to settle down, love a man who can respect me. But where would I find such a man? Who would respect what I've done?"

Tears were streaming down her cheeks. She ignored them. "You made me realize that, Jack. Not until you walked out that night did I really know what was important and wasn't. You get into a thing here in Hollywood. It's a merry-go-round, spinning and spinning until you can't get off, and you don't even realize you want off until it's too late. I was so desperate when I went to see your uncle, I'd have done anything to get out of the situation I was in. And he knew it. And used it. And suddenly I found myself doing that damned film, then I was drugging myself with booze and didn't really know what was happening any more. And I continued to be emotionally numb, walking without feelings, without caring any more. Your uncle took the guts out of me.

"And you—you put them back, made me look a second time. You start living the lie with people who are in the same shit hole, and you don't actually realize what's happening. You know, but you don't know, because it would be insane. And the night when you rushed out of the room, I knew what I was and had to prove to you that I wasn't cheap and...like that. Maybe you were only a symbol...representing the bloody world. If a man like you could have such contempt—"

He laughed at that. "A man like me?"

"Well, you know what I mean," she sounded desperate.

"Yes. I do. You aren't the only one that's dirty. You aren't the only one that made mistakes. We both have dirt in our faces. So we're not perfect." Johnny covered her lips with a finger.

"Just perfect messes! Right?" There was a hint of humor to that, yet her voice was filled with such self-contempt that he hugged her gently to him for a moment.

As they parted, he offered:

"You know why I came here to Hollywood?"

"Not really."

"To escape the dirt I'd made of my own life. For years I'd been living off rich women—prostituting myself. So, I ran out. Came here." Johnny laughed bitterly. "And look at the crap I fell into!"

They were silent again, this time trapped in their own world of thoughts.

She wasn't the only woman who had gone down this ugly road. It didn't have to be a dead end. He had heard about a very famous actress who had started out doing stag movies. But she had found fame and love, and men who accepted what she had become. And her sordid past was now a meaningless event having little to do with her present life.

Looking at Jean, Johnny suddenly realized that maybe he'd been wrong, unfair to her. Love was a strange, yet wonderful emotion that could forgive all. And, he realized, it didn't matter what a girl had been in the past—it was what she was in the present. And what she could become in the future.

Both of them had stepped down a shitty pathway; it was time they changed course.

Suddenly, without ever knowing how it happened, he had pulled her into his arms and was covering her lips with tender kisses. There was nothing sexy about it; this was love, total emotion.

Every emotion played its part as they embraced. Every nerve seemed to fire in a beautiful love pattern. This was totally different from pure passion or lust.

Johnny sensed a different, more meaningful pleasure.

Their kisses lingered, caressing more than their lips, their bodies, literally enveloping their total beings.

After awhile the two of them stood and walked into the bedroom. They undressed quietly, then slid down onto the bed. He folded his arms around Jean and held her gently, tenderly caressing her head against his chest.

"I don't know, Jean," he said in a soft whisper, "but maybe we should forget the past—maybe we should start over, at least find out what we do have, what we can have together."

"Oh, Jack. Jack. You mean it?" She moved to look up him, her eyes filled with happiness.

Johnny was surprised by what he had said. Now, with her so close, he found the reasons for not allowing himself to love her were becoming weaker and weaker.

"Hell, I don't know," he cursed, crushing his lips against hers. He didn't want to think about the feelings tormenting his mind and emotions; he didn't want to do anything but escape, to become physically drunk with her body. In passion he might be able to forget, to stop thinking, to be only aware of sensations and nothing more.

And as their bodies blended, as she greedily opened her whole body to him, he suddenly wanted to give to her more than he had ever given to another woman before. He wanted to weave a web of wonderful sensations through her nerves. to caress her in such pleasure that all the inner torments that had made her own life a hell would be momentarily washed away.

It all happened like some lovely fantasy as they seemed to fold about one another, embracing, tenderly kissing. He didn't even want to go beyond those beautiful sensations. All that counted was holding her in his arms, being aware of the soft, velvety texture of her skin, the warm cushion of her body pressing gently against his. They were suddenly captured in a new universe, a place special only to them, a dimension beyond the physical world, yet very much physical. They seemed to be blended together, like two souls becoming one. And that, in the end, generated a magnificent flush of desire that demanded attention, that surged about him in wave after wave of pure electric energy. He was flooded with her, with his love for her, with a kind of totally overwhelming need that surpassed any other need he had ever known. Even if, in the end, the actions were no different from those experienced with other women, endless times, it was different. And that difference was what he needed to capture into his very heart and soul for eternity.

When they finally strained together for the last time, one thought kept blasting away inside his head: *God! I love her!*

Slowly he slipped away from Jean. She was lying there, exhausted in the aftermath of their love-making. He was certain that consciousness had slipped from her.

Johnny rose from the bed and went into the living room. He sat on the couch, torn by the thoughts raging through his mind.

When he made love to Jean, all he saw was a woman wanting love, wanting understanding, wanting respectability. And in that he saw the mirrored image of himself. Not until now had Johnny realized that love had any place in his life. Not until now had he known that he had been searching for love, for understanding, for a place, emotionally, in the world for himself. And against that, all else was unimportant. Where he worked, or how he made his living, became merely an action necessary to perform for material survival; the important thing was *why* he worked. Suddenly he had a reason for living, a reason for working, a reason for existing.

The sound of Jean's footsteps coming toward him jarred Johnny out of his thoughts. He looked up and there she stood, naked and beautiful, in the middle of the room.

"I never knew it could be like that," he told her. "I never realized what it was like."

She merely smiled and then slid into his arms. "I

love you, Jack. Love you more than I've ever loved anything else. I don't give a goddam what happens, where this ends, but I want you for as long as you'll let me have you—on your terms, with your rules, anyway you want. Just let me love you!"

Johnny kissed her lips, kissed her eyes, her cheeks. She lay her head down on his lap, looking up into his face. His hands caressed over her whole body. They didn't say anything; words weren't necessary.

Johnny knew he was in love with Jean. He knew was all that mattered. The past was unimportant; the future distant and without shape. But he was in love, and enjoying it. Loving being in love with Jean Harold.

He forgot about Laura and he forgot about everything except his need and love for Jean.

The rest of the night was a melody of love which drew them deeper and deeper into its all-embracing arms.

The next morning Johnny was jarred awake by the ringing of his telephone.

He looked down at Jean, who was lying next to him, then leaned over and kissed the soft red of her lips.

Getting up, he rushed to the phone.

"Yes?"

"Jack, Laura."

Johnny tensed. Sweat broke over his body. He'd forgotten all about her.

"What is it?"

"Ben's gone for the afternoon. I want to come over." Johnny hesitated. He had planned on spending the afternoon with Jean; he had planned on never parting from her, as long as that wonderful feeling continued between them.

"I can't, Laura."

"What do you mean, you can't?" she snapped. "I'll be over in a couple of hours."

The phone went dead.

Johnny stood there for a moment and then slammed the receiver on the hook.

Going into the bedroom, Johnny woke Jean by kissing her lips, hard and passionately this time.

Her arms slipped around his neck. Her voice murmured softly, wordless sounds of love.

"We gotta get out of here," he told her.

"Why?" She frowned.

"No questions. We can go to your place. How about it?"

"Some other girl hounding you?" she asked laughingly.

"Yes. Quite frankly."

Alarm clouded her face. "Gloria?"

"No."

"Who?"

"Laura Henderson." He felt sick inside. Standing, he started gathering his clothing. "She's been after me ever since I came to town."

There was a coarse, ugly groan from Jean as she got off the bed. Her arms gripped his shoulders, turning him around.

"What is she to you?" she demanded.

"Nothing. Nothing at all. I wish she'd drop dead!"

Jean grinned and then shrugged. "Don't be such a killer!"

He smiled and patted her cheek. "Let's split out

of here before it's too late."

* * * * * * *

Laura arrived at the club half an hour after Johnny started work that night. She wore a dark blue dress that dipped low in the front and flared at the skirt. She came up to him at the bar and sat down.

"Hello, nephew," she greeted casually.

Johnny grunted, awareness of her presence made him gulp on the drink in his hands.

"You aren't in a very friendly mood," she observed.

"Do you think it was smart, you coming here?" Johnny asked.

"What's wrong with visiting my nephew?" she whispered, lighting a cigarette. "You're a bastard for running out on me this afternoon."

"I had company," he told her.

"Gloria or Jean?"

"Why don't you ask the girls?"

She shrugged, as if it didn't matter. "There'll be an end to that, soon."

Johnny jerked around to face her for the first time. "Get off my back, Laura."

"Oh, you wouldn't want me to do that, would you? I need you," she hissed in his ear. "Let's get out of here. I want to talk to you. Real serious like."

"Not interested."

"Yes you are. You better be. This is serious business. And I mean it!"

He considered her words, attitude, then said: "I don't think we should be seen leaving together."

Laura shook her head.

"Ben wants to see you, Johnny," she announced in a loud enough voice so that the bartender could hear.

With a sigh, Johnny stood. The two of them left the club.

Once in Laura's car, she drove down the street. They were quiet for a long time. Finally she said, "Okay, Johnny, let's have it out!"

"I think we better stop—while we're ahead," Johnny announced.

"I love you Jack. I have to have you."

"You're married."

"I'm going to divorce Ben."

"You're kidding!" Johnny exploded.

"Why? Why not? We're good for each other, you and I. We're alike. We fit. I never knew what love was until I met you, Johnny. I thought I loved Ben, but I realized it was the money. Last night, when he made love to me, I wanted to vomit. I couldn't stand being touched by him. I can't take any more of it. I'm divorcing him. I'll be free. We can—"

"Oh, for God's sake, Laura! Cut it out. It's been fun, but I love somebody else."

"It's Jean Harold, isn't it?"

"None of your business!"

Laura slammed on the brakes. The car skidded to a stop in the middle of the street. She whipped around to face Johnny.

"I want you. I'll have you. Nobody else gets you, Jack. I mean that. I can't live with any other man. I can't stand another man touching me. I love you. Don't you understand? I'll be a good wife to you. We fit. We're good together."

Johnny took a deep breath. Then forced himself to say, "I don't want you. Can't you understand that? Can't you get that through your head? It was fun—while it lasted. But it's finished. Whether you like it or not!"

With that, Johnny opened the car door and got out. He sprinted to the sidewalk and then started down the street. He didn't look back to see what Laura did.

It was the sound of her car starting, then turning around, that caused him to look.

The car speeded toward him, the headlights blinding. Sweat broke from every pore in his body.

There was only one possible way to avert death. He waited until the last moment

But it wasn't necessary.

Laura turned the car just before it would have crushed his life away. The auto banked, halted for a moment, then shot down the street.

* * * * * * *

Laura's mind was screaming insanely. She knew that the emotional wall that had been built around her life had suddenly cracked.

As she drove home, she realized what she would have to do. If she couldn't have Johnny, nobody would. She would finish him off, for good. But in a way that wouldn't send the law down on her. She had almost driven over him.

An hour later she was sitting in the living room, drinking, smoking, and nervously pacing the floor, waiting for Ben Henderson to return home.

God, how she hated Johnny, her mind kept yelling over and over again. *No man had turned her down flat like that.*

But now it was all quite simple. Quite easy. Now she would get rid of two troubles, two thorns. Once Ben knew what Johnny had done to her, once Ben learned that his young nephew had forced her into a sexual act, he'd be after Johnny. He'd take care of Johnny for good. Fix him so nobody would want to climb into his bed. Maybe even make it impossible for him to have sex. One nice castrating slice and Johnny's love life would be fixed for good. No more lover boy; no more living off rich ladies; no more cheating on her.

And the law would take care of Ben Henderson.

Laura laughed as she thought about it.

Then the front door opened and Ben Henderson walked into the living room.

CHAPTER TWELVE

Johnny found a phone booth and called a cab. It was about twelve-thirty when he returned to the club. As soon as she was able to, Jean pulled him aside. Her face asked all the questions.

"I don't think she'll bother us again," Johnny assured her.

"You're white," she announced, alarmed.

"She tried to run me down, but turned at the last moment," he told her. "Laura's a strange woman."

"What if she did something else—told Ben Henderson—"

"That would get her in just as much trouble. Gloria found out and threatened to expose all to Uncle Ben, if Laura didn't put in a good word for her on the stag movies. The woman thinks that's a career move. Porn star. Christ! Laura almost had a nervous breakdown at the very thought of Ben learning things about her…" He left it at that.

"No," Johnny said thoughtfully, "she wouldn't do a thing like telling Ben."

"See you after work, Jack?" Jean asked.

"Of course, honey. We can split. You don't work tomorrow, do you?"

She grinned. "Not a minute.'

164

"I'll tell Carter I'm cutting out. How about skipping to the mountains?"

Jean nodded and then returned to her customers.

It was late in the morning by the time they started for Big Bear Lake.

They had stopped off at both of their apartments to pick up some clothing. The only thing that kept them from making love was the thought of letting the excitement and need build higher by waiting until they had gotten to the lake.

The unexpected spur-of-the-moment trip had keyed Johnny up. All thoughts of Laura and what she might do had washed away. For a day and a night they were free from all possible complications. They would be alone, and have a chance to find more about each other, to explore the beautiful emotions that had bound around them.

It was about eight-thirty when they arrived at Big Bear Lake. As tired as they were from the long trip, they didn't waste any time getting undressed, slipping into bed, and locking in a passionate embrace. Afterwards they lay there in each other's arms, aware of the intense emotional bond that held them.

"I never loved a man before, Jack," she murmured in his ear. "What with all the, well, wanting to be in pictures and what followed, I didn't have time. Life gets you on a roller coaster and you just ride, hanging on, desperately trying to avoid flying of into space. And maybe I didn't know what it was I wanted until you came along."

"Let's not talk about it. I don't want to think about the future. I don't want to think about anything except right now."

Jean snuggled closer.

Sleep clouded around them. When Johnny wakened, Jean was still clinging in his arms, her breasts rising and falling against his side, in rhythm with her breathing.

He looked at her.

She was the loveliest sight he'd ever seen. It was more than just a physical thing, it was the whole of Jean that was beautiful.

Johnny tried to picture her the way she had been in the stag film, but couldn't make it. All he would see was another woman, another person that wasn't really Jean at all. Nothing but light and shadows on a screen; an acted out film scene without any meaning or reality to it.

Slowly he leaned over and caressed her lovely breasts. The he gently kissed them.

"That feels good," she murmured in a sleepy voice.

"I didn't mean—"

"Shut up and make love to me," she laughed.

The morning and afternoon blended in the sensations of their love. It was late in the evening before they finally got up and dressed. They went out and ate and then returned to the motel to find the softness, the warmth and love of each other.

Johnny kept telling himself it was all insane, all madness, pure madness; but every time he held her, he knew that he would never tire of Jean, he knew that he would never want to leave her, he knew his life would be empty and useless without this lovely woman.

He would somehow get the pictures she'd made from Ben Henderson; some way manage to have them destroyed.

When he awoke the next morning he wasn't surprised to discover that he still felt the same way about Jean.

Turning and leaning over her, he kissed her lips. Jean stirred and then opened her eyes. She smiled, and the expression held all the love, all the emotional tenderness that he was feeling.

"I still love you, Jean," he murmured, smothering his lips into the hollow of her throat.

A tremor shivered through Jean, and she clutched him tightly to her.

Suddenly, as if controlled by another being, unable to stop himself, Johnny said, 'How about us making this a permanent thing?"

Jean's face brightened, but her lips asked, "What kind of an arrangement are you talking about?"

Johnny laughed. "What kind do you think?"

"I don't want to think; I want to know."

"Get married—husband and wife—the whole works."

She was serious, thoughtful for a moment. "You really mean it, Johnny?"

"I never meant anything more in my life!"

Jean came into his arms, hugging close. And in moments they began making love again.

The trip back to Los Angeles was a clouded daze of happiness. That afternoon they planned on getting their marriage license.

He drove to his apartment, dizzy with love and excitement. They parked outside in the street, then went up to his apartment.

As he opened the door, Johnny had the first

sense of danger. Voices came from behind the door.

He tensed, then stepped into the room.

Joe Carter and another man, a stranger, were sitting on the sofa.

"What's going on?" Johnny demanded. "What are you doing here?"

Joe Carter grinned but the hatred that burned in his eyes almost stunned Johnny.

"Mr. Henderson wants to see you, Johnny!" Carter announced, pulling out a gun. "He wants to see you right away." Carter nodded to the other man. "Mac, phone the boss."

"What's the meaning of this?"

"Just sit—and don't ask questions." The grin was filled with sadistic pleasure. He motioned with the gun.

Johnny felt sweat prickle through his body. It had something to do with Laura, he knew that much. It had to be that.

"Come on, Jean," he said, moving to the sofa and sitting down.

Why, his mind screamed. *Why?*

He didn't want Laura; he hadn't really ever wanted her. All he needed now, or would ever need, was sitting down beside him. Jean Harold.

Somehow he would have to make Ben understand. But there was a small terrified voice that screamed over and over in his mind that it would be impossible.

He glanced at Carter. "This really isn't necessary."

"Oh, but I think it is. About time the big stud lover got his! You think you can stick it with any lady. Well, you did one too many. Now you're getting yours!"

He stared to say something, then decided against that. Carter was literally enjoying himself. The man was petty and dangerous.

But he didn't matter. He wasn't the real danger.

Ben Henderson wasn't the type of man to merely shake off the affair with Laura.

It was a long wait; a long wait of silence. The only thing that Johnny was aware of was his thoughts, and the tiny, delicate hand that clutched his.

Finally the door opened, and Ben Henderson burst in, Laura behind him.

His face was livid with hate and rage. Laura was calm, her right eye darkened by a bruise, her lips swollen. But she was dressed, as usual, in high style. Beautiful, even in her condition.

"What's the meaning of this?" Johnny demanded, standing, deciding to play dumb and see exactly how things stood.

"Shut up, you little shit! Just shut up!" Ben jerked forward and his fist slammed out, smashing into Johnny's face.

Johnny felt the bridge of his nose give, and the trickle of blood slowly start down into his lips.

"I should kill you, Johnny—kill you!" Ben stood over him like a mountain of seething flesh and fury. His eyes blazed in raw hate. "Laying my wife! You dirty son of a bitch!"

Johnny glanced at Laura. The expression in her eyes was bright, excited and full of hate.

"You know what kind of woman Laura is?" Johnny inquired, staring evenly at his uncle, controlling the emotions that were choking up inside him like a steel spring about to explode.

Ben's hand slashed out, snapping Johnny's head to one side.

"Shut your filthy mouth!" Ben demanded. "Just shut your filthy mouth!"

Johnny glared at his uncle. "Why don't you either get out of here or do what you came for?"

Ben Henderson blinked. He took a step back, and stared. Johnny said, "I don't care what you believe, Uncle Ben. But if you asked around, maybe you'd discover a few things about Laura. I didn't want anything to happen, regardless of what Laura told you, and—"

Ben moved so fast that Johnny didn't have time to protect himself.

He heard Jean scream.

A hard fist slammed into his stomach; he doubled over and met another blow that knocked stars into his eyes, smashing him down onto the sofa. He was sick for a long time. An acid tasted in his mouth, but he swallowed it down; his eyes burned with tears, his lungs gasped for air.

Finally the red mist cleared. He looked up at Ben Henderson

"What...what…do you want?"

"To fix you for good. Real good, sonny boy. To fix you so that you never do anything like that with a woman like Laura. She told me how raped her—and the way you used the first time to make her continue. And the way you—"

"That's not true!" Johnny said in a shocked voice. He looked at Laura pleadingly.

She merely stared back; only her eyes were bright with hate.

170

Johnny felt Jean slide away from him. He looked at her.

"Please—that's not true. It happened, she wanted it, it happened and I tried to stop it. Believe me, Jean. I don't care about anything else. You just believe me."

Jean's features struggled with themselves, and he could see in her eyes the frantic wanting to believe.

Then Laura stepped up to Johnny. "You filthy degenerate beast! Don't try to lie you way out of this!" She turned and looked at Jean. 'We've all done some dirty things, but the first night Johnny was with me, he tried to get me to bed. Then, after the party, he raped me. Raped me violently. I can show you the bruises, if you want to see them. He really did a good job. Then, later, he forced me—he did some terrible, dirty things—real dirty!"

Her acting was magnificent. Even Johnny was stunned by her performance.

Maybe he had deserved this; maybe it was his punishment for the life he led during the past years. A punishment for a degenerate and depraved life. Most of the time he'd had contempt for the women involved; not caring anything about them other than as a meal ticket.

All at once Johnny sat up straight, amazed. It was the first time he'd ever considered himself actually bitter towards women. It was the love that Jean had inspired in him that had brought the realization to the surface of his mind. The hate for his mother.

Now, for the first time in his life, Johnny felt a heavy burden lifted from his shoulders. It was as if freedom had been offered—a freedom that even his love for Jean hadn't completely given him.

It was guilt; guilt at what he'd been. Now that he understood, he could forget and forgive. Like he had learned to forget and forgive Jean for what she'd been.

Johnny looked up at his uncle. The man was standing there, a grim tightness pounded on his features, hate burning in his eyes.

"I don't know what you have in mind, Ben, but I think if you consider it, it's not worth it. I'm leaving town anyway." He looked at Jean. "With her, if she still wants me."

Jean hesitated only a moment and then nodded.

"We want out, completely out. You can do what you want. If you truly believe what happened, what Laura said happened, then do what you will."

Johnny stood and faced his uncle.

For a long time they stood there silently staring. Then Ben Henderson turned and looked at Laura. Then he nodded toward Carter and Mac. "Do what you came to do. Take him out of town, and see to it he's fixed for good, so he can't have women any more! Break his guts. Have a doctor cut him so that damned prick can't work—got me?"

"No!" Jean cried, horrified. She stood and came between Johnny and Ben Henderson. "No! You can't do that. You can't ruin everybody's life just because you—"

"You slut—shut up, or you'll end in the hospital too."

Jean stepped back. "I wouldn't do it, Mr. Henderson!"

Henderson glared at Jean and then laughed.

"You can't do a thing about it, and you know it. Just be glad I didn't call some of the real toughs. Johnny would have ended up real bad, in some lake, or the ocean. He's part of the family. I want him punished, nothing more. Just fixed for good!"

Jean said, "Don't touch him, Mr. Henderson, or I'll tell the police about your filthy porn racket!"

Henderson's face went chalk white. His lips parted to say something, but Johnny stepped between them.

Then the man simply laughed. "The police? I own them…are you kidding?"

"No, you don't!" Jean announced. "You don't scare me any more. There are decent people in the world—and this town, nation, society, won't put up with your kind running people's lives, perverting us…you're not God!"

"Fix her, too!" Ben nodded toward Jean. "You guys take care of her—for good! Kill her!"

"Kill me, too, you bastard!" Johnny said, "You'll have 'cause if you so much as touch her, I'll kill you!"

There was a long, stony silence, a silence that was terrifying as Ben stared at his nephew. Then suddenly the man let out a deep, tortured sigh.

"What do you want, Johnny? I can't let you get away with all this crap. What you did to Laura—"

"If you believe her lies, you're a bigger ass than I would have thought possible," Johnny announced. He didn't care any more and there wasn't anything to lose. "She's just a female Johnny Belton. Don't you see it? She slept her way into a marriage for money and position and power and to be kept. I know. And damn it all, if you'll get your big ego out of the way you'll admit the truth. She's lying. She seduced me. She wanted to play. She's been cheating on you from the first. You can find that out if you want to face the truth. Whatever lies she's fed you are because I ended things…I tried to end them before they got started. I was wrong to go even that far. But you know her talents—and if you're honest you'll admit it. She's hot. Sure. A lot of women are. And she's very good at seducing a man. She uses her body for favors. Just like I did. Face it!"

There was a very long silence as the expression on the older man's face shifted from grim hatred to anger to realization. He glanced at this wife.

"He's lying!" she screamed.

"No…" Ben said, softly, "I don't think so."

"For God's sake, Ben—I'm your wife!"

"You're a paid slut," the man countered unemotionally. "I knew it from the beginning, but didn't care. Then I started to believe the lovely fantasy. So…I'm just another sucker for a fancy…never mind." The man's eyes turned to Johnny. "Okay. We're related. I don't like what you did with her…but fair is fair. You're blood. I'll respect that. What is it you want?"

"To be left alone—to have you give me all the prints and negatives of Jean's films. We'll destroy them, later."

Another silence. Then: "Okay. But don't ever, as long as you live, have anything to do with me. Don't call or write or anything!"

Laura screamed and rushed forward, ripping the gun from Joe Carter's hand. She swung around, leveling it at Johnny. She screamed at the top of her voice: "If I can't have you she won't!"

Ben was the one to move. His actions were amazing for a man his bulk. One arm whipped out smashing Laura's head to one side.

The sound of thunder exploded in the room; an explosion that shattered from one wall to the other.

Ben Henderson staggered back, his face drained, his mouth sagging, his eyes bulging, tormented in pain and shock. Then he slowly slumped to the floor.

Johnny recovered first and quickly disarmed the stunned Laura. He pointed the gun toward Carter and instructed Mac to call the police.

The long wait that followed was a torture of suspense.

* * * * * * *

The next months had been hectic, but Johnny managed to get the films and negatives from Larry, Ben Henderson's partner, before the law was able to close down their racket, after Laura had told everything she knew about Henderson in a plea bargain. She would spend a long time in jail and be an old woman before she was free again.

The day was hot, blazing from the California summer sun, when Johnny and Jean stepped out of the Los Angeles Court House and walked down the street to where he had parked his car.

Even the thought of the trip ahead, the long haul to Las Vegas, where they would be getting married, couldn't cut away the sadness of the last hours.

Jean sensed his mood and was silent until they were in his car.

"Look, Johnny," she said, squeezing his hand

and gazing into his eyes. "She got what was coming to her. They said it might be a very short time. The doctors will help. After all, it was only manslaughter. And they had that sanity thing. Buck up, honey—we have a wedding to go to!"

She smiled and hugged closer.

Johnny looked down at her and was amazed, for the millionth time, at the emotional love that welled through him.

They had both come up out of the gutter, cut their past bonds, and were now facing an uncertain future. But they had a new start.

"Afraid, honey?" he asked, starting the car. The depression was already beginning to fade. The court seemed far away.

The past seemed already gone. There was only the future.

Jean laughed and moved closer so that he could put his arm around her shoulder. "I'm not afraid with you, Johnny. I don't care what kind of struggle we'll have. After what we've been through, everyday living, loving and struggling will seem like child's play."

Johnny found the freeway, then headed east. It would be a good five to six hours before they reached Vegas, but it was the road to their future, and with each mile the past would be that much further away.

They would take their time, and when the day ended, it would be the close of the past. In the morning a new volume would have begun, as Mr. and Mrs. Johnny Belton.

It was already getting dark by the time they reached Vegas. And the next morning, a little past eleven-thirty, they had started the first scene of their new life, together, as husband and wife.

ABOUT THE AUTHOR

Charles Nuetzel was born in San Francisco in 1934, and writes:

"As long as I can remember I wanted to be a writer. It was a dream I never thought would materialize. But with the help of Forrest J Ackerman, who became my agent, I managed to finally make it into print.

"I was lucky enough not only in selling my work to publishers but also ending up packaging books for some of them, and finally becoming a 'publisher' much like those who had bought my first novels. From there it as a simple leap to editing not only a science-fiction anthology, but also a line of SF books for Powell Sci-Fi back in the 1960s. Throughout these active professional years I had the chance to design some covers and do graphic cover layouts for pocket books & magazines."

Much of his work in covers and graphics are a result of having had a father who was a professional commercial artist, and who did a number of covers for sci-fi magazines in the 1950s and later for pocket books—even for some of Mr. Nuetzel's books.

In retirement he has become involved in swing dancing, a long time lover of Big Band jazz. But more interestingly world travels have taken him (and his wife Brigitte) across the world, to Hawaii, Caribbean, Mexico, Kenya, Egypt, Peru, having a lifelong interest in ancient civilizations. His website is full of thousands of pictures taken during these trips.